The gold ring inside the velvet box had a diamond that, in the right light, was large enough to signal satellites. Eadie snapped the box closed and stood up to lean across the table and set it in front of Hoyt.

Hoyt sat back in his chair to stare at her. He looked stunned. Well, so was she. And maybe insulted. If this was a joke, it was a rotten one she never would have expected from him.

"Your ring is beautiful," she said casually. "But who's it for...?"

Susan Fox lives in Des Moines, Iowa. A lifelong fan of Westerns, cowboys and love stories with guaranteed happy endings, she tends to think of romantic heroes in terms of Stetsons and boots.

Fans may visit her Web site at www.susanfox.org

HIS HIRED BRIDE

Susan Fox

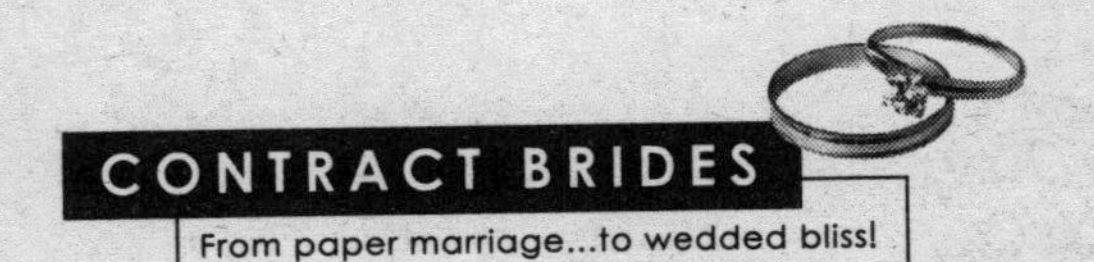

TORONTO • NEW YORK • LONDON
AMSTERDAM • PARIS • SYDNEY • HAMBURG
STOCKHOLM • ATHENS • TOKYO • MILAN • MADRID
PRAGUE • WARSAW • BUDAPEST • AUCKLAND

ISBN 0-373-18194-9

HIS HIRED BRIDE

First North American Publication 2005.

This edition published by arrangement with Harlequin Books S.A.

www.eHarlequin.com

Printed in U.S.A.

CHAPTER ONE

THESE days, Eadie Webb was almost the only person in their part of Texas who got along well with rancher Hoyt Donovan.

Eadie managed that by either staying out of his way or by treating him with relentless good grace. She ignored his surly expressions, bore it patiently when he was terse or blustery, and pleasantly accommodated his every dictate.

She knew precisely why he was out of sorts lately, and it tickled her sense of justice, though she'd never confess that to him in so many words. Partly because she was too polite to do so; partly because she didn't want to take the chance that she might somehow hurt his feelings.

Men like Hoyt never owned up to having feelings anyway, at least not the kind that could be hurt, so any truthful remarks she might make about his situation would only enrage him further and increase the misery of everyone who happened to cross his path.

Hoyt Donovan was the most god-awful male chauvinist in Texas, and though he deserved to suffer some sort of consequences for his actions, no one else deserved to suffer with him. Not that Eadie believed he was truly suffering like normal mortals would, but he'd probably had his pride dented. And pride—particularly male pride—was all important to men like Hoyt.

But then, he'd come by that pride naturally. His blunt, stony looks gave him a rough handsomeness to go with his earthy sensuality, which was patently unfair for females like her who were too lackluster to ever enjoy anything more of them than the view.

Because of his rugged good looks, Hoyt Donovan had been the target of every marriage-minded female in their part of Texas, and women flocked to him like butterflies. If he wasn't in the mood to have his male vanity catered to at that moment, he was arrogant enough to send them scattering with a cranky look or some other, more subtle indication of disinterest.

He could be bad about that, but it didn't

seem to make a lasting difference to the butterflies. More taken by surprise than offended or hurt, they recovered quickly and came fluttering back for another chance. He seemed somewhat more attracted to the mercenary ones, and they were usually the ones he put up with the longest, as if he enjoyed an occasional challenge to his unrelenting date 'em and drop 'em style. He deserved something for that, but his dating habits were more a by-product of his biggest flaw.

He didn't treat his women badly, and none had ever complained that she'd heard about. He periodically sent them flowers between one expensive date and the next, and he almost always sent them a decent piece of jewelry or some interesting trinket after he stopped calling them. Eadie's only problem with his generosity was that Hoyt regularly assigned those chores to her, and she'd been put in charge of the actual selections.

It wasn't that he didn't show his women a good time, because he did. He knew how to treat a woman like a queen, and he had a diabolical knack for catering to a lady's interests, whether those interests were his or not.

But his ability to dictate the emotional parameters of the relationship, yet remain remote and unmarried, was becoming the stuff of legends. He'd left a prodigious number of broken hearts along his trail, so if he was surly now over finally getting jilted by the one woman he'd actually taken seriously, he deserved it.

But the biggest reason Eadie Webb hoped Hoyt Donovan would suffer a bit longer, was that his male tastes ran—no, *galloped*—to beautiful women, and always the most beautiful ones. He liked leggy blondes with haystack hair and puffy lips, exotic brunettes with lush curves, and fiery, green-eyed redheads who wore their costly designer clothes two sizes too small.

He didn't seem to notice that most of his beauties were more self-involved and shallow than he was. Until he'd finally met the one who'd done him dirt.

Eadie felt ashamed of herself suddenly. She not only owed Hoyt her gratitude for hiring her to work for him a few afternoons a week, she also owed him her complete loyalty and deference because of a discreet act of kindness he'd once done for her. Though neither of them had ever spoken about that awful night since or even vaguely referred to it, Eadie felt the bitter-sweet burden of obligation to him.

Perhaps one of the reasons she felt so little sympathy for his upset of late was that the gentle man—the supremely kind man—he'd been that night five years ago, had been appearing less and less frequently these days. There'd been times this past year when she'd found his sour moods increasingly obnoxious, and she often wondered if she'd dreamed what he'd done for her way back then.

What no one would ever know and what Hoyt Donovan would never suspect, was that she'd fallen in love with him that night five years ago. Completely and irrevocably. Because she had, and because she was the very last woman on earth that beauty-obsessed Hoyt Donovan would ever consider a romantic possibility, Eadie was fully aware that the biggest reason she took such a harsh view of his love life was that she couldn't seem to get past the jealousy she felt, so it gave her more than a little satisfaction to know he'd gotten a taste of his own medicine. She wondered if the beautiful Celeste had sent *him* a ‘‘parting gift.’’

It frustrated her that Hoyt couldn’t see that his beauties were too in love with themselves to ever truly love him. Hoyt wasn’t a stupid man, and she’d always been wary of his insights, but he was as dense as a brick on some subjects.

Five years of loving him in secret was a long time. Long enough to prove, even to her, that Hoyt Donovan’s tastes would never change. It hadn’t taken five minutes for Eadie to realize he’d never be interested in a plain woman like her, though it had taken her far less than five minutes that awful night to realize she was doomed to love him—almost unconditionally—for the rest of her life.

Eadie forced herself to ignore the depressing sense of hopelessness she felt as she finished tidying up Hoyt’s desk. She’d typed his letters and caught up on his bookwork, saving it all to files before obsessively backing them up. Donovan Ranch was a monstrous headache to keep track of. Her three afternoons a week made a respectable dent in the paperwork, but Hoyt took care of the rest himself.

He'd paid her well for the tasks he'd hired her to do, and the money came in handy on her own small ranch, though the extra income evaporated by the time she got done paying bills. If things at home continued going downhill, by next year she might have to sell out.

The notion dragged her spirits lower. The idea of having to move to town and take an office job was traumatic. Aside from losing touch with the ranch life she'd loved and had grown up with, she'd no longer have either a reason or the opportunity to see Hoyt, though that was probably for the best. At twenty-six, the only thing more pitiful than being doomed to achieve ''old maid'' status in another few years or less, was to hang around a man she could never have.

The sound of Hoyt's heavy bootsteps pounding steadily through the big ranch house startled her and she automatically glanced at the clock. The fact that Hoyt had apparently come back to the house early today wasn't a good sign, not when he was still so riled and cranky. Because his bad mood had grown worse this past week, Eadie had taken greater pains to stay out of his way. She'd hoped to make her escape before he came back to the house, but his sudden arrival thwarted her plan.

From the bedroom end of the house opposite the wing the office was located in, she heard him thunder, "Eadie? I need you in here! Now!"

The order was as angry as she'd ever heard, and Eadie hurriedly finished stacking the handful of letters with their envelopes on his desk blotter to rush out of the room. Hoyt never leveled his bullish temper on her, though he often treated her to a blustery verbal account of the reason for his choler. She suspected he did that because she always listened calmly, and her very calmness seemed to cool him off by the time he was done letting off steam.

And of course, once he finished, he usually saw reason and quickly got over his aggravation. That was one of the things that made her forgive those times when his temper rose high: when he cooled off, Hoyt was truly mellow, and he didn't hold grudges.

The problem in the aftermath of his

breakup with the beautiful Celeste was that he'd fumed around for weeks now, and as far as she knew, he'd not spoken more than a handful of choice words on the subject. Most of what she knew had come from gossip. Which was why she'd guessed that his male pride had somehow been soundly assaulted. And why he wasn't showing signs of letting go of a bit of his anger over it anytime soon.

She'd barely made it down the hall and halfway across the big living room before he bellowed out another, "Eadie—get in here!"

She sprinted the rest of the way across the living room to the hall, suddenly shaky because she sensed something new about his anger this time.

As she slowed to rush into what had to be the master bedroom, her shaking increased. She'd never been in the private areas of Hoyt's home, and his bedroom was the most private. And intimate. She had only a moment to note the dark luster of the wide headboard of his massive bed before she reached the open door of the master bath and rounded the corner.

The moment she saw him, Eadie realized

that for the rest of her life, she'd always feel this same wild excitement and rush of happiness at the mere sight of the man.

Hoyt was so big and broad-shouldered, his powerful, work-hardened body the very zenith of masculinity. His larger-than-life presence made the large bathroom feel about a foot wide. Beneath the black Stetson he still wore, his hair was dark and overlong, and his face was almost too rugged and harsh to be considered handsome, though it was.

And she adored him. Truly and simply, Eadie adored everything about Hoyt Donovan, though she'd never in a million years confess that to him or to anyone else. She'd taken brutal pains to make sure she never showed it.

The glittering black gaze that missed so little when it wasn't dazzled blind by female beauty, arrowed straight to her heat-flushed face and impacted her startled blue gaze with enough force to make her eyelashes give an involuntary spasm.

"It's about time," he growled. "I coulda bled to death in here."

Alarmed, Eadie's wide gaze dropped to the side of his ripped and bloodied chambray shirt as he turned, then pulled the shirttail out of his jeans and held it up to display the oozing slice in the hard flesh beneath.

Eadie's gasp was overridden by his clipped, "Hurts like a son-of-a-gun."

His remark was far less profane than it might have been if he'd been talking to one of his men, but Eadie barely noticed as she stepped close for a better look.

"You need to see a doctor."

"Medical stuff's in the cabinet right there." He nodded toward a panel of the wide mirror that spanned the long counter. "Clean me up an' slap on a patch."

Hoyt's voice was loud in the crowded space. His frustration was in the terse order, but the volume of his voice was anger. None of it made much of an impression on Eadie because she knew instantly that his frustration was with the injury and his anger was at himself for being injured in the first place.

"It needs stitches," she said as she quickly washed her hands, hastily dried them, then rummaged briefly in the cabinet he'd indicated to find antiseptic and sterile gauze pads.

"You too squeamish to do it?"

The demand was a bit more crabby than angry, and they both knew she was anything but squeamish. Eadie opened the peroxide, then tore open a few of the sterile pad packs to dampen them. She turned toward him to brush the pads gently around the gash to clear away the blood, and answered.

"There's a big difference between cowhide and your hide."

"Stitches are stitches. If you can sew up a cow, you can sew me up."

Eadie let herself smile faintly to acknowledge how ridiculous that was. "Not the same thing," she murmured as she continued to work.

"How come?" Now his big voice had gentled a bit more as if his temper was already cooling.

Eadie glanced up to make eye contact. "Your hide's thicker."

As she'd hoped, he'd liked that. The lingering anger in his gaze abruptly softened to a glitter. The stern line of his mouth curved slightly. "Do tell."

Eadie looked back down at her work, thrilled, flustered, but confident it wouldn't show. She'd had years of practice keeping her face blank, even when Hoyt got that dangerously sexy look that made her ache for him. She knew that sexy look wasn't aimed at her for any special reason. It was just the man's natural state, and nothing to take personally. She directed them both back to the business at hand.

"Let me finish here and cover it, then I'll call the doctor and find someone to drive you to town."

"I'll drive myself," he growled, and Eadie wasn't surprised. As long as Hoyt was conscious and on his feet, she wouldn't think of arguing with his macho declaration. He'd consider the suggestion polite, but arguing with him about it would somehow put his manhood in question.

"Suit yourself."

The silence as she gently worked suddenly seemed odd somehow. There was a tension to it, but the tension could only be hers. After all, taking care of Hoyt like this was a tiny spark of heaven. And that was not only ridiculous, but evidence of how pitiful she was.

Helping Hoyt with paperwork was one thing, but cleaning the small wound on his side seemed intensely personal, at least for her. She was tingling all over and her insides were fluttery. And oh, *oh,* she loved even a flimsy excuse to stand so close to him, and she couldn't get enough of the smell of leather and sunshine and man.

Meanwhile Hoyt wouldn't even notice the smell of her bargain shampoo. He wouldn't be any more affected by her touch than he would have been if someone had absently brushed against his arm in a crowd. Though she knew that, the longer this small bit of first aid went on, the more intense the tingles and flutters became.

She couldn't help it. Touching him, even like this, was about as good as it got for her. And Hoyt's skin was not tougher than cowhide. It was hot and firm on his side, surprisingly silky, and the steely muscle and bone beneath were rocklike. Eadie suddenly felt a primitive feminine craving to touch more of him.

"How come your hands are shakin'?"

The blunt question made her heart jump and Eadie felt her face go a scorching red. She tried to cover it with a faked hint of irritation.

"You stomped in bellowing for me like

a crazed bull. And since cleaning this has got to hurt, I keep thinking you'll bellow again."

"That all it is?" There was something edgy in his stark question, as if her trembling hands had somehow put him on alert and made him suspicious of her.

Which seemed like nonsense until it dawned on her why he'd go on the alert. Considering Hoyt's taste for beautiful women, even a faint hint that sexless, Plain-Jane Eadie Webb might be getting a bit excited over this was sure to be a horrifying notion for a lady-killer like Hoyt.

Hurt by the idea, Eadie tried to finish quickly. If he'd suspected enough of her feelings to hint so fast that he was repelled, then it was time to counter his impression by rushing this. The doctor would insist on doing a more thorough job anyway, but for now it was clean enough to cover for the ride to town. At least the bleeding had almost stopped.

Eadie tossed the last wad of soiled gauze pads into the sink, then reached for three of the larger gauze packs to tear them open. In moments, she had the big squares pressed against his side and took his hand to lift it to hold the pads in place so she could tape them.

But taking Hoyt's big, callused hand was like taking hold of the live end of a broken powerline, and Eadie couldn't tell if her reflex was to yank her hand away or to hold on tighter. When she guided his fingers into place over the gauze pad and let go, her racing heart slowed a good ten beats per second. As desperate to deny the snapping charge she'd just gotten as she was to get this over with, she briskly tore off strips of tape to anchor the pad to Hoyt's skin.

When she finished, she took an extra second to press a ripple of tape more securely against him. Only she had to know that the ripple was no ripple, but was instead an overwhelming need to touch Hoyt one last, daringly insane time. In the normal course of her life, there'd been few opportunities to ever touch him, and she was certain this time was destined to be the last.

Eadie reached for a small dark green towel and handed it to him. "Take this along, in case it starts oozing."

She gingerly reached for the corners of the soiled gauze pads and bent to get out the small garbage can from beneath the sink. She transferred the squares to the trash before she put it back under the sink and let the door close. She'd just turned on the hot water tap to wash her hands and squirt some liquid soap from the ceramic dispenser into her palm before it dawned on her that Hoyt was still standing close by, not moving away as she'd expected.

Eadie sneaked a peek into the mirror to confirm what she could already see in her peripheral vision. Hoyt was staring solemnly at her, watching her every move. Her gaze dropped back down while she briskly washed her hands, splashed a bit of water against the bowl of the sink to rinse away any spots, then turned off the faucets and stepped away to dry her hands.

She'd not wanted to allow herself to read something ominous in Hoyt's profile as he'd stared at her, because the fact that he was staring at her couldn't be good. Though her instinct was to get out of his sight as soon as possible, she tried to sound cool about it.

''Well, that's it,'' she said, taking a moment to straighten the hand towel on the bar as she automatically did the same with the larger ones next to it. Clearly Hoyt wasn't the neat freak she was. "Be sure to ask the doctor when your last tetanus shot was in case you need another. I was just about to get home."

With that, she turned to walk to the door without looking directly at him, but Hoyt caught her arm. The fresh jolt that he gave her sent her gaze shooting up to his.

"That's it?" His dark brows were cranky whorls that confused her.

"I said I'd call the doctor."

"You're gonna let me drive to town alone?"

Eadie studied his stern face a moment, unable to miss his disapproval. "You said you'd drive yourself."

"You'd let me do that? I thought women liked to fuss."

Eadie gave her head a disbelieving shake. "Do you…want me to fuss?"

He released her arm then and growled, "Not if you have to strain yourself."

Eadie stared harder, unable to grasp this, though she was almost amused by it. "So you do want me to fuss," she concluded as she tried to come to grips with the idea. "How much fussing…would you want?"

She almost giggled over how ridiculous

that sounded, but didn't dare. Hoyt looked deadly serious!

Now some of his stony expression eased and a bit of the ire in his dark eyes died down, as if her question mollified him.

''Considering how froze up you are, slather it on. I'll let you know if it's too much. My side's stingin' like a son of a buck, and it feels like you cleaned it with acid.''

Eadie ignored the crack about her being ''froze up'' and instantly felt bad that she'd hurt him. She impulsively touched his arm. ''I'm sorry. Can you walk to my truck or do you need help?''

''I can walk,'' he grumbled, then added, ''just steady me till we're sure.''

Genuinely sorry she'd hurt him and anxious to make up for it, Eadie took back the hand towel and moved to his uninjured side. She helped him lift his arm as she ducked beneath it so he could rest it across her shoulders and lean on her if he had to. She hesitantly put her arm around his waist and got a grip on his belt, both to avoid coming in contact with his injured side but also to provide a hold in case his legs somehow did give out.

That idea seemed absurdly far-fetched because Hoyt was so physical and naturally strong, but if he was feeling poorly enough to sacrifice a little male pride to ask for assistance, then he must be feeling bad. He hadn't nicked an artery, but maybe he was a little shocky. Could he have hit his head?

"You're a puny little thing, you know that? How the hell do you do outside work?"

Eadie turned her head to briefly look at him before she faced forward to start him toward the door. He didn't sound weak, just irritable. Looked it, too.

"Thanks for the compliment. I don't have to be big to use smarts. Lean on me if you need to because it's almost closing time at the doctor's. You don't want to pay for the emergency room," she said as they walked out into the bedroom.

"You're supposed to coddle me, not worry me about money," he said, vexed.

"Sorry."

"And it sounds like you don't think I'm worth the extra fee."

Eadie tried to be patient with that surprising hint of self-pity. It was out of character. "Money's an automatic worry for me,'' she said calmly. ''I forget some folks don't need to worry.''

''That's right, it's *my* money,'' he said, then went on. ''But how come you worry? Are you saying I don't pay you enough?''

''It'll be easier to coddle you if you stop talking.''

''I never noticed meanness in you before, Eadie Webb.''

She couldn't help an ironic smile, since he couldn't see it. ''I'm not surprised.''

''Why aren't you surprised?''

He was like a child who couldn't stop asking questions. Eadie was patient with him because his relentlessness might be a cover for genuine pain. ''You've got better things to do than make a study of me.''

''Do tell,'' he said, and the way he drawled it the slightest bit made her smile again. ''Maybe I ought to use my convalescence to make a study of you. What do you suppose I'd find out?''

Oh, Lord, what was this about? Her smile faded. It was about nothing, *absolutely* nothing. She'd do well to remember that.

''If you were studying me now,'' she said, suddenly inspired, ''you'd figure out that I'm beginning to doubt you need me to lean on."

"You think I'm fakin'?"

"Yes, and I wish you wouldn't. I've got a sink full of dishes and chores in a couple hours, so if you don't really need me, I'd just as soon get home."

"What if I paid you overtime?"

"I wouldn't take pay for something like this."

"Then I reckon I could do your dishes later."

Eadie giggled over that. "Would I have any left that weren't broken?"

"I'd buy you a new set. And a dishwasher, too."

"I've got a dishwasher, but I can't use the extra water. Please, let's just get you to town."

Eadie got him to the front door then had a brief argument about whether they'd take her little truck or his big new supercab pickup. She gave in for the sake of time and helped him into his truck before she rushed to the driver's side and got in to start the engine and get the air conditioner going.

She turned to get out and dash to the

house to call the doctor, but Hoyt vetoed it. ‘‘Miss Ed should already have done it, so let’s just go.’’

So Hoyt had been putting her on, at least about wanting her to stitch him up instead of a doctor, since the call to the doctor had already been made. She closed the driver’s side door and adjusted the seat so her feet could reach the pedals before she put on her seat belt.

‘‘Your legs are short.’’ Hoyt’s brusque observation made her smile a little as she put the big truck into gear.

‘‘Thanks so much for all the fine compliments, boss. I’m puny, my legs are too short, I’m mean. And let’s don’t forget how ‘froze’ I am. Keep that up, and you might turn my head. Of course, that might be just before you got dumped along the highway someplace.’’

‘‘Huh. Those are not coddle words, Edith Regina Webb.’’

‘‘No, they aren’t,’’ she said and flicked a glance his way. ‘‘And you’ve sprung a leak. Better put that towel over it and apply some pressure.’’

Eadie faced forward and pushed down on the accelerator to rocket down the long driveway to the highway. Once she got on the pavement, she settled back and tried to enjoy the novelty of driving a nearly new pickup with a powerful engine that all but flew them to Coulter City.

CHAPTER TWO

HOYT got right in at the doctor's, since they'd arrived just before Doc Harris finished with his last patient of the day. Eadie was surprised when Hoyt asked if she was going in with him. He'd said he wanted her to go in to help him keep the doctor's instructions straight, but Eadie was suspicious of that. She went along though, torn between the pleasure of being needed and the feeling that Hoyt was somehow toying with her. He seemed as hale and hearty as usual, so the fact that he wanted her to go in with him was odd.

No sense trying to figure this out, though. Eadie sat down on a chair out of the way and tried not to be conspicuous while the nurse took his vitals, noted them on his chart, then went out. Whatever reason Hoyt wanted her in here, it was sure to seem strange to the doctor.

And maybe suspect. After all, Hoyt was

a known ladies' man who'd had a parade of women through his life. Eadie was his lackluster, part-time secretary who not only worked three afternoons a week for him, but had now trailed into a doctor's private examination room with him. Eadie felt no small embarrassment over how that might look to the doctor. Would he think she was imposing on Hoyt to get his attention? Eadie suddenly decided she was willing to risk Hoyt's ire by leaving him alone in here.

And of course, the doctor came in just as she stood to go to the door and slip out. He eyed her like some unusual phenomenon.

"Well, hello to you, too, Eadie," Doc Harris said as he peered at her over his half-glasses, his kind eyes lively with curiosity. "Is there some interesting development between you two?"

Eadie's face went red-hot. "H-Hoyt... just wanted me to—to come in and get your instructions straight, but I don't need to do that until you finish with him."

The doctor looked at Hoyt. "Do you want her in or out while I have a look?"

"In."

The terse little word was nothing less than an order, and the doctor grinned.

"She stays then. Let's get that shirt off and see what we've got." He spared a moment to send Eadie a glance. "Might as well have a seat, Eadie. Right over there's fine."

Eadie felt another tide of fierce heat wash into her face and hesitantly went back to the chair to sit down, but kept her gaze fixed on the floor as Hoyt took off his shirt. Doc Harris adjusted the table to an incline so Hoyt could sit back. She could tell the doctor was carefully pulling away the gauze patch. And then she heard it hit the nearby tray as he discarded it.

"Ah well, it's just a nick," the doctor scoffed. "I thought we had something serious here. Eadie could have fed you an aspirin and sewed you up in a flash. Or called the vet."

Eadie's gaze flew to the doctor's grinning face, then realized he was making light of Hoyt's injury as a tease. After all, the gash was almost four inches long, and it was oozing again. Eadie realized then that this was a typical joke between macho males. Doc Harris would have made the same remark if Hoyt had come in with his leg half cut off. And she could tell by Hoyt's rugged profile that he was grinning almost proudly. *Men!*

The doctor went briskly out, leaving the door open. Eadie took a steadying breath, tried to stay where she was and not stare at Hoyt's bare chest. Doc Harris came back fairly soon and his nurse trailed in after him with a stainless-steel tray that she exchanged for the one with the discarded bandage.

Doc dismissed his nurse, wishing her good-night, then took care of everything himself. All the while, the two men talked cattle and markets as if they were doing no more than chatting over coffee. Eadie was relieved that they both seemed to have forgotten she was in the room, but she was aggravated to be present for this.

What a ninny she'd been to allow Hoyt to put her in this position, and yet she couldn't entirely blame him for that because a large part of her couldn't help giving in to him. He'd truly wanted her in here, whatever his reason, and she couldn't help thinking again about that time years ago when he'd come to her rescue.

The two situations weren't even remotely alike, except that what he'd done for her in her time of trouble and need had automatically guaranteed that she'd never refuse to come to his aid during his time of trouble or need. She'd just never considered that his trouble or his time of need would be so relatively minor. She hoped they'd all be this minor.

In truth, being in here with Hoyt gave Eadie a strong taste of what it might be like to be entitled to be with him in things as small as going to the doctor. If she were a wife instead of an employee, she'd get to share a multitude of things like this, along with happier things.

And that was just more proof of the shameful fact that she was pathetic enough about Hoyt to grab for every crumb that fell to her, however much her pride squirmed and screamed at the indignity. On the other hand, depending on how things worked out with her little ranch in the next few months, her pride might have at least some hope of relief if she decided to sell out and move to Coulter City. She'd be doing that sooner rather than later if some unforeseen financial crisis popped up.

It took a moment for her to realize the doctor was waving his hand to get her attention.

"I thought you were supposed to listen to my instructions?"

Eadie cringed a little. "Sorry. I was thinking about something else. When was his last tetanus shot?"

The doctor's smile widened. "Good question." Then he winked at Hoyt. "Is she always that good at keeping track of you?"

"I'm just a weekly paycheck to her, Doc," Hoyt complained, though his dark eyes glittered with amusement.

"I'll look up the date, but I'll call in a 'script to the pharmacy for an antibiotic and a painkiller." He looked back over at Eadie. "He'll need to take the antibiotic till it's all gone, of course. Make sure he takes it with food. No booze with the painkiller. No driving. And keep him off machinery and horses while he takes that one. Stitches out in seven days."

The doctor peeled off his latex gloves and discarded them, then washed his hands. He went out as Hoyt gingerly rose to a full sitting position. Eadie got up and retrieved his shirt to hand it to him.

''Help me with this, would you?'' he said, and Eadie sorted out the sleeves and helped him put on his shirt, careful to accommodate him to keep his movements from pulling on the flesh around the stitches.

But, oh, the foolish and dismally unforgettable pleasure of helping Hoyt with a task as casually intimate as putting on his shirt! His hard body was so wholly masculine that her insides quivered like jelly. The fact that she couldn't avoid having the backs of her fingers brush against his hot skin here and there was another pleasure/torment.

Hoyt at least buttoned his own shirt, but didn't tuck it back in. ''Do you mind running me to the pharmacy to pick up the medicine or do you have to get home?''

''We've got time for that,'' she said as she belatedly forced herself to step back, feeling a little chastened for her earlier declaration that she had dishes and chores to do. She did have to do those things, but there was still plenty of time to keep to schedule, thanks to the doctor's quick work.

He came back in then with a syringe and a small vial. "Eadie was right on the money about the tetanus shot. It'll probably ache worse than the scratch on your side." Now the doctor gave Eadie a sparkling glance over the top of his half-glasses. "You might want to step out for this one, since it'll go in his hip."

Eadie nodded, only too glad to comply. That would have been even more over the top and unnecessary than being present for all the rest. She took refuge in the waiting room until Hoyt came out. They walked to the pickup but there was no discernible sign of weakness in Hoyt at all. When they got to the pharmacy he went in by himself while she waited. It wasn't long before he'd come back out with a small white bag and they were on their way back to Donovan Ranch.

"My thanks for your help, Eadie," Hoyt said, and his mood seemed mellow and almost pleasant. She hadn't seen him like this in weeks, and got the idea that coming with him to Coulter City might have helped do that.

It was a dangerous notion though, and close to lethal to think that she could have a mellowing effect on Hoyt. Yes, her calmness usually did have a strong effect on him, but he'd been particularly difficult lately, and she'd seemed to have lost the knack. When he'd come to the house this afternoon, he'd been even more impossibly cross and difficult than usual. Remembering that made her realize his good mood now might be solely because his bad mood had simply burned itself out.

They'd just got to the Donovan Ranch driveway and turned onto it when Hoyt broke the pleasant silence.

"Miss Ed's probably gonna go home at her usual time tonight. Is there a chance you could come back after chores to set me up for the night?"

Shocked, Eadie glanced over to see the dead seriousness about him. And there was just the faintest impression that he was cradling his side but trying not to be obvious about it, as if, despite the truck's cushy suspension, the light vibration from the graveled driveway made him uncomfortable but he was too macho to let on.

Eadie glanced back at the road ahead and

gently slowed the big truck in hope of minimizing his discomfort. Now that it had been a while since he'd got the injury, it was probably making itself sharply felt. The local anesthetic had surely worn off, and his side had suffered not only the injury, but the trauma of being stitched.

Yes, he probably was genuinely hurting now. Eadie glanced at Hoyt a second time to see him silently watching her, his dark eyes unreadable as he waited for her to reply.

Her soft, ''Of course I can,'' made him give a grim nod so she faced forward again. There'd been no sign of teasing in his gaze this time, no hint that he was putting on.

Of course I can she'd said. Eadie suddenly knew then that she'd always do whatever he wanted, whenever he wanted her to. Heaven help her, she'd probably be saying *yes* to Hoyt Donovan or *Of course I can* for the rest of her days.

She was like an old-time cowboy who swore allegiance to the brand he rode for, and lived it out come hell or high water until the day he died and was planted under the sod in the ranch cemetery. The dreary knowledge dragged her spirits low.

* * *

Before Eadie headed back to Donovan Ranch, she had a quick bite to eat, took a shower and washed her hair. She applied a bit of makeup before she dried her hair and put on a good pair of jeans and a yellow cotton shirt. Eadie would never wear either the yellow shirt or her single pair of designer jeans to work outside, and both were a nice change from what she wore every day of the week except Sunday and special occasions.

It wasn't a big change from her regular jeans and work shirts, which she also wore to do paperwork at Hoyt's, but it was something. And she'd gotten her shower out of the way because she wanted to be ready for bed when she got home. The only thing left to do was wash her face and go right to sleep. Morning came early at 4:00 a.m., and tomorrow would be a long day.

Tonight would be something out of the ordinary for a workday night, and Eadie felt too foolishly excited about going over to help Hoyt to be sensible about this. Though she was a hopeless case where he was concerned, she would at least be dressed a little nicer tonight and feel good about the way she looked while she was being an idiot.

Eadie knew she didn't look bad. She was plain, but not unattractively so. Her blue eyes were standouts because of her light tan and her dark, shoulder-length hair. She had even features and a nice smile. In truth, she'd always been happy about the way she'd looked.

Until she'd fallen for Hoyt. Knowing about his taste for beauties had caused her to compare herself with some of the most spectacular women in Texas, so of course she'd come off looking as plain as an unpainted fence to herself as well as to Hoyt.

She hoped she at least had a nicer personality than some of Hoyt's women. He'd always seemed to like her well enough. But then, he also liked his housekeeper, Miss Ed, so his liking wasn't proof of anything in particular. Miss Ed was no beauty herself, but Hoyt hadn't hired her to hang around his house looking beautiful.

Though the very sour Miss Ed was a good woman, she had anything but a Miss Vivacious-Never-Met-A-Stranger personality. Hoyt had hired her because she took care of his house the way he liked and she was a peerless cook, so she got along with him fine.

Eadie got along with him fine, too, despite his prickly moods. He seemed to enjoy talking to her, venting his complaints, getting her opinion, and he appreciated the way she handled the things he'd hired her to do for him. Beauty and sparkling wit were irrelevant, though Hoyt sometimes seemed at least charmed by her.

Eadie suspected he'd enjoyed their little exchanges today, and in retrospect it was more than a little flattering that he'd made her a part of everything after he'd got hurt. She ignored the idea that he currently had no adoring beauty to call on, and because it had been nearing closing time at the doctor's office, most of his beauties wouldn't have had time to come to the ranch to demonstrate their sympathy anyway.

And Hoyt had asked *her* to come over tonight. There was no getting around the fact that she'd grown even more excited about the out-of-the-blue opportunity the past three hours. Despite her effort to keep her head, Eadie just couldn't seem to keep from losing it yet again over Hoyt. Hope probably did spring eternal because she was surely the most hopeful—and hopeless—ninny on the planet.

Even picturing a disappointing scenario didn't seem to put much of a damper on the lighthearted way she felt. She had no business expecting anything but more crabbiness from Hoyt tonight, and she was certain to face a complete and utter letdown over how ho-hum it would all turn out to be.

But for now, she felt happy. She checked the clock about a half dozen times before she figured it was late enough to start for Donovan Ranch. She went out and got in her little green pickup and once she'd made it up the ranch road to the highway, she had a hard time keeping the little truck enough under the speed limit to avoid getting a ticket on the ten-minute trip down the pavement.

When she finally pulled up to the front of the massive, single-story adobe-style Donovan Ranch house, she noted that Miss Ed's ancient little car was indeed gone. Though it was just before sunset, a few lights were on here and there in the house.

She went to the front door and pushed on the doorbell, then waited for Hoyt to answer it. When he didn't, she pushed the button again, then waited even longer for a response. Finally she realized he might have taken the painkiller and fallen asleep somewhere in the house. He couldn't have gone to bed and left the lights on, so she debated whether or not to just go on in.

Though she'd worked for Hoyt for years now, Eadie never simply walked into the house unannounced, though she'd had permission to do so. She regularly arrived just after noon, so she always went around to the kitchen and tapped on the big glass patio doors to get Miss Ed's attention before she came in.

Could Hoyt be in trouble? She certainly didn't want to startle him if he just hadn't heard the doorbell, but she was squeamish about just walking in. Leery but concerned, Eadie tried the knob and the door opened easily, so she walked in and called out a light "Hello."

When she got no response, she closed the door, then crossed the stone floor of the foyer to the long, carpeted hall that spanned the length of the big house.

"Hello, Hoyt. I'm here now," she called out, then hesitantly started down the hall toward Hoyt's office, peeking in doors on her way past only to find that the big den was empty. She went in and turned off the lights, then came back out and started through the house.

The kitchen and dining room were immaculate, but empty, as was the living room. She glanced out to the big patio in back, but there was no sign of Hoyt. Then she saw his black Stetson hanging on a wall peg in the dim kitchen, and was certain he had to be in the house. Eadie started toward the bedroom wing.

The only light in this part of the house was coming from Hoyt's bedroom, so she stopped just short of the doorway to rap her knuckles on the door frame without looking in. If he'd just stepped out of the shower in the altogether, she didn't want to compromise his privacy. There was no response, but she heard what sounded like a soft snore.

Eadie cautiously peeked in and saw Hoyt sprawled on his back on the big bed. He had on a fresh shirt that he hadn't tucked in and a different pair of jeans than he'd had on that day, but he was fully dressed. His boots were on again, so perhaps he'd laid down earlier because he was drowsy then had fallen asleep. Surely Miss Ed didn't know about this, because she might have given him heck for putting his boots up on the beautiful bedspread.

Eadie couldn't let him sleep the night in his clothes, so she started across the carpet to the big bed to touch his shoulder.

Her soft, "Hoyt, can you wake up?" was a whisper. She gave his shoulder a gentle nudge. "Hoyt? It's Eadie. You need to wake up and get ready for bed."

That seemed to rouse him and he began to stir. But the unguarded movement must have hurt because he drawled out a swear-word. Eadie decided she had to be a little more firm and spoke in a more normal tone.

"Hoyt? You need to wake up. Be careful of your stitches, but wake up." She gave his shoulder another nudge. "Hoyt?"

His low moan was more a resistant growl than an indication of pain, so she reached for his fingers and, careful not to brush his injured side, which was facing her, she chafed his hand between her palms.

And...oh, Lordy! The feel of his big,

callused hand between hers was a guilty pleasure she didn't dare indulge too long.

"Come on, Hoyt," she coaxed, almost as much to get him to wake up so she could let go of his hand as to spare him an uncomfortable night. "You can't sleep in your clothes. Wake up so you can take them off and get under the covers."

The low growl that answered her was a shock.

"You take 'em off."

Eadie stared down at Hoyt's sleep slack face, stunned. She'd stopped chafing his hand between hers and that next second she realized her mouth was hanging open. Had she heard right?

CHAPTER THREE

HOYT had mumbled something to her, but the words had sounded distinctly like *You take 'em off.*

Replaying it in her head didn't change a syllable, and—*hooboy!*—that was the last order she'd ever dreamed Hoyt Donovan would give *her.* She must have heard it wrong.

"H-Hoyt? You need to wake up and get your clothes off for bed."

This time, the growl was more distinct. "I *said, you* take 'em off if you want 'em off so bad."

Eadie felt a tickle of amusement over that even as her face went warm. "I will not take your clothes off, boss. Just get up and get it over with. It shouldn't take more than a minute, then you can go back to sleep. Come on."

She pulled on his hand a little to prompt

him to rise, but his dark eyes sprang open and zeroed in on her.

"You should have got here before I fell asleep. Now it's gonna hurt like hell to get up again."

Eadie smiled sympathetically. "I'm sorry. Here," she said as she leaned close to slide her other hand beneath his wide shoulders, "I'll help you sit up."

Eadie knew it was a mistake the moment she felt the heat from his body penetrate her clothes. The hard muscle definition of his shoulders instantly imprinted themselves on her arm and palm and fingers. To pay back a little extra misery for her good intentions, the spicy cologne she associated solely with Hoyt filled her nostrils and was mildly intoxicating at this distance.

Hoyt's fingers tightened on her hand. "You'll help me sit up, huh? You and what forklift?"

His minty breath gusted warmly into her face and Eadie struggled not to show her reaction. "Are you calling me puny again? I'm also wiry."

That got a smile out of him, but Eadie had underestimated the appeal of it happening just inches from her face while she was bent over him.

"You're wearing perfume."

The raspy pronouncement embarrassed her and made her regret her earlier efforts. The last thing she could afford money-wise and pride-wise was for Hoyt to think she was after him. And she rarely wore perfume.

"That's shampoo. I washed my hair."

"That why you're late?"

"Let's get you on your feet," she said, then did her best to lift him.

Hoyt released a gusty breath, but cooperated. Once he was upright, Eadie tried to pull her hand from his, but Hoyt didn't release her.

"Hold still. I need the balance," he growled as he slid his legs off the bed and put his booted feet on the floor.

Eadie felt excitement storm through her as her hand stayed in his and she stared down at him, but then she rallied and tried to be all-business.

"Did you start the antibiotic?"

"Done. And the other about an hour ago. You up to getting my boots off?"

Eadie could see the weariness about him,

so she couldn't refuse. "I suppose." One corner of his mouth bent down with displeasure.

"If you're gonna go balky on me, I can use the bootjack."

"I can do it." Eadie pulled her fingers from his and stepped back to reach down and get a grip on his left boot.

"You make me feel like a pest, Eadie," he groused as he lifted his foot to help her.

"I don't mean to," she said and pulled the boot off. "You've got to admit though, that our business deal never involved things like this before." She set the boot down then went for the other one.

"I thought you said you wouldn't take pay," he went on in the same grumpy, aggrieved tone. "Does that mean there's only business between us with no friendship or neighborliness at all?"

Eadie pulled off the second boot. "Of course there's more than business between us," she said as she picked up the other boot and set them both out of the way. "I apologize for making you think otherwise. I wouldn't be here if I didn't care about you, Hoyt."

"That's a relief," he said, though he

sounded anything but relieved. "But it's hard to take it personally when you care about everybody."

There was a strong hint of self-pity and maybe frustration in the way he'd said that, and Eadie made a desperate try to ignore it. After all, Hoyt wasn't quite himself, and who knew how the painkiller was affecting him?

"How do you really feel about me, Eadie?" he asked quietly, and everything inside her went on full alert. "I haven't exactly been easy to get along with lately."

The admission got her by the heart. It was an acknowledgment that he'd been difficult. And the way he'd said it was also an admission of regret. But she didn't dare answer the question that preceded it. Not with the truth.

Eadie might have been able to find some way to overlook his question and focus only on the second part of what he'd said about not being easy to get along with. She was ready to say something that might lighten things up and get a grudging smile out of him.

The words to do just that were on the tip of her tongue, but then his gaze lifted to hers, and the solemn look she read there not only got her by the heart but squeezed hard. The subject neither of them had spoken about or hinted at for five years was suddenly between them, and Eadie felt compelled to break a little of that years-long silence. The time seemed right, and perhaps Hoyt did need to hear this from her.

"Even if you're never easy to get along with again, Hoyt," she began softly, "there was a time in my life when you did something for me I'll never forget. No, I don't like the way you've been lately, but I know who you really are deep down. That's the man I'm here for tonight. I might do just about anything for that man."

Eadie felt her heart leap into a panic over the starkly candid confession. She was certain to regret it, but the somberness about Hoyt tonight had brought out the fool in her. Then again, her feelings for Hoyt had steeped in secret for so many years that it wasn't much of a surprise she'd let a little of them come out just now. Tonight was something completely new between them, and it was affecting her in dangerous ways.

If revealing even that tiny bit of her feelings to Hoyt made him order her out of his life and never show her face again, it might be a mercy. Five years was a long time, a pathetically long time.

The seconds ticked past as they stared at each other. Eadie couldn't maintain the contact, so she glanced away. "If you'll stand up, I'll turn down the covers for you. Then I'll get out of here so you can get ready for bed." She made herself look at him again. "You do have everything you need for the night, right?"

"I'll make do."

His dark gaze was pressing deeper and deeper into hers, so she glanced away to reach for the top of the bedspread. As she'd hoped, that prompted him to stand, so she briskly pulled down the spread and top sheet before she turned to him.

Even in his sock feet, Hoyt towered over her, and he'd never seemed bigger or more blatantly masculine than in those hushed seconds next to his big bed. And sexy. The man oozed it.

"Well, I...need to get home. I'll see you Tuesday, as usual, unless you need me for something before then." She glanced up into his face then away. "Take it easy, and mind the doctor. I'll call Miss Ed tomorrow to see how you're coming along."

"You won't stop by tomorrow to check on me yourself?"

Eadie was as threatened by the question as she was pleased. "What about…after supper?"

"Why so late? Is tomorrow a big workday for you?"

"Yes." It truly was, and now she was a little relieved it would be. She needed some perspective, and hard outdoor work was good for that.

"You've still got folks workin' for you?"

Eadie shrugged, uneasy with the question. "I've been trading off chores. I've got work at Junie's in the morning to pay back help, then work of my own when I'm done there."

"You hurtin' for money?"

Trust Hoyt to just bluntly ask, though it was a shock that he had. Eadie was starting to hurt for money more than she was comfortable with, though no one but her needed to know.

"Not that it's any of your business, but I just have to cut extra costs. I'm still making up for inheritance taxes. Nothing earth-shattering."

No, not earth-shattering, but more like a cliffhanger. Eadie hated to lie, but she was ashamed she hadn't been doing better the past few months. Small ranchers had a hard time, and she was grateful she only had herself to support. Nevertheless, it wasn't something she wanted Hoyt to know about.

"If you need something...well, you know I'm good for it."

Apparently Hoyt's antennae were up, because he didn't let it drop. She needed to draw a polite line to ward him off, because she considered the subject of her money troubles highly inappropriate.

"That's kind of you, thanks. And generous. But I can stand on my own."

"I mean it, Eadie."

A small smile burst up from the combined dismay and tenderness that was all but breaking her heart. "I know."

She dared to touch his arm. "Thanks." Eadie barely resisted the urge to let the touch linger. "Do I need to lock up on my way out?"

"I never lock up. The dogs take care of

varmints. It's more entertaining than locking the doors."

Eadie gave a laugh. Hoyt's dogs were the laziest hounds in that part of Texas. They loved kids and women, but they lived for strangers. Their god-awful baying was more than enough to alert the ranch, whatever time of the day or night.

They barely paid attention to her comings and goings, so if she saw much of them at all, it was when she took a moment to pet them on the back patio on her way in to work, or when Hoyt had them in the den. And that was rare because Miss Ed didn't like dogs in the house.

"All right then," she said. "Good night."

"I'll walk you out."

Eadie shook her head. "You will *not* walk me out. I've been walking out of this house alone for years now, so I think I can remember the way. Get your clothes off and go to bed."

Hoyt gave her a narrow look. "You're bossier than I ever thought."

Eadie's brows went up. "You *need* bossing more than *I* ever thought. Good night now."

Eadie didn't give him another chance to delay her. Standing by Hoyt's big bed in the soft lamplight had put enough pictures in her brain that she'd have to blot out, along with the ones of him shirtless in the doctor's office.

She made her escape, but just outside the front door she nearly tripped over Mike and Mose, who were sprawled like roadkill just outside the front door. Eadie took a moment to bend down to give them a pat.

"So you two do set up a sentry after dark."

Mose rolled over for a belly rub and Mike did the same.

"Some watchdogs you are," she scoffed with a laugh as she briefly accommodated their shameless appeal. When she had, she straightened. "Back on duty, boys."

Both dogs whined as she went to her pickup and got in, but they subsided quickly enough and went back to their usual watchdog postures. Which was to lie flat on their sides like lumpy, long-eared rugs.

Eadie did take a minute at lunch that next day to call Donovan Ranch to check on

Hoyt. Miss Ed filled her in, because Hoyt had company. Eadie tried not to jump to the conclusion that his visitor was a woman, but since Miss Ed didn't say who the company was, she'd gotten the impression that one of Hoyt's women had dropped by. Could it be the beautiful Celeste?

News traveled fast in and around Coulter City, and the doc had seemed amused that Eadie had been with Hoyt so he might have mentioned it to his wife. Someone was sure to have noticed that Eadie was driving Hoyt around in his new pickup. Since Hoyt never let a woman drive, that would have been noticed faster than anything else.

Hoyt had also gone into the pharmacy by himself, bold as you please, wearing his ripped and bloody shirt with the white bandage peeking through the gap in the cloth, so no doubt everyone knew about that by now, too.

Clearly one of his former girlfriends or possibly some potential new one had come by to look in on him. That meant Eadie wouldn't need to bother. She'd been the gap-girl yesterday afternoon and last night, since Hoyt was between women, but perhaps her time doing that was already done.

By the time Eadie finally finished her work and her usual evening chores, she was filthy, fatigued and famished. There was leftover roast in the refrigerator that she'd craved for the past two hours, and there was enough that she wouldn't have to cook.

She was hot and sweaty, and she was still itching from the hay chaff that had been stirred up by the breeze coming through a loft window that had somehow come open. She'd not wanted it to keep flapping, so she'd made a quick trip up to close it, then got caught in a swirl of chaff that had gusted off the loft floor as she'd reached the top of the ladder.

But that was the least of her problems. She was greasy from a frustratingly long encounter with the tractor that had been elderly when she'd graduated high school over eight years ago. It was acting up yet again, an almost weekly occurrence, and Eadie didn't want to think about how much it would cost to fix this time. Whatever was wrong with it now was beyond her modest mechanical abilities. She'd have to get someone out to have a look, because it was a cinch she'd never be able to make payments on a loan for a new one. Or even a used one. Since she used it regularly enough, borrowing someone else's was out of the question so a repair was her only choice.

It was things like those and a half dozen other little problems that day that made her wonder how long she could continue on. Eadie had faced hard times before, both when her widowed mother had been alive and they'd done most of the work themselves, and later when Eadie had made a go of things alone in spite of the inheritance taxes she'd had to come up with after her mother had passed away six years ago.

That had been crippling enough for someone who was land rich but cash poor, but she'd held on with the help of a loan, though it would take another four years to pay it in full.

If she hadn't loved ranch work and country life so dearly, she might have sold out years ago and moved to town. Eadie shunned the thought most of the time, but there were days like today when the thought was hard to reject. Particularly now, when her energy was spent and her fighting spirit felt faint, and it seemed like nothing in life would ever get appreciably better.

The sooner she sold out, the more money she'd have to pay things off and buy a place in town. If she had to give up the small ranch before it went broke, it was smarter to get out in time to be able to buy a house outright and pay cash so she'd never again have to worry about a bill higher than a modest car payment.

It was a big decision, and she couldn't ignore her emotional connection to the place, though she'd be better off if she could. Her father had saved half his life to buy it, then had worked himself into an early grave trying to make it pay. Her mother had given it her all, too, so Eadie felt compelled to ride out the troubles and try to think of some way to get the ranch into the black.

Tomorrow she'd try yet again to come up with some other solution. If all else failed, maybe she could sell off some of her herd and lease some land out. The problem with that was the water situation. The cost of putting in a couple of deeper wells had been a little too steep for her limited resources the past three years, and still was. But if the weather improved enough to take their part of Texas a little farther away from near drought conditions, her problems with water might ease.

Eadie couldn't seem to let go of the endless mental search for solutions as she dragged into the enclosed back porch, hung up her Stetson on a wall peg and walked over to the washer and dryer that took up half the small porch. Knowing there was no one around for miles to see in the windows that faced the barn out back, she pried her boots off on the bootjack, then started to take off her clothes to put right into the machine.

What she had on would fill out the load she'd been building in the washer this week, and all she'd have to do after her shower was come back out to add the soap and start the cycle. She could dry the load in the morning if she couldn't stay awake long enough for it to finish tonight.

She'd already vetoed the idea of going to Donovan Ranch to look in on Hoyt. He'd just have to be happy with a phone call. If his visitor that day had been a woman, no doubt she'd be the one tucking him in tonight anyway, so a quick phone call would be more than enough.

The pounding that suddenly started at the front door made her groan. Whoever it was could just go away, she didn't want company. But then the pounding came again and it sounded insistent enough that she knew whoever it was would eventually come around to the back and knock again.

Only the way her luck was going, they'd probably show up just in time to catch her in the raw. Eadie stayed where she was as she waited to hear the sound of a vehicle start out front and then drive away. She unbuttoned a couple more buttons, hoping…hoping…

But then she heard bootsteps on the stone walk out back, and her heart gave a little leap as she recognized that booted stride. Hoyt's big voice was muffled by the enclosed porch.

"I brought you a hot supper. Are you gonna let me bring it in?"

Eadie looked up at the porch ceiling and called out, "You're supposed to take it easy."

"Miss Ed made you one of those chocolate pies you like so much," he called back. ‘‘The fancy stuff on top’s about to make a mess.’’

Eadie couldn’t help a tired giggle before she resolutely rebuttoned enough buttons to be decent before she turned and walked to open the porch door. She knew the moment she saw Hoyt’s face that he was shocked by the way she looked, so she gave him a tired smile.

‘‘Can you bring it in by yourself, or do you need help?’’

‘‘I got it this far,’’ he said tersely, then nodded toward her clothes. ‘‘Go do something with yourself while I bring it in.’’

Well, that was certainly tactless, and Eadie couldn’t help another tired half smile. The smile wasn’t because of the grumpy remark that hinted Hoyt was a little shocked by her filthy and bedraggled appearance as much as it was because it was so wonderful to see him, too wonderful. Whatever his mood, Hoyt would always be the stuff of spinster dreams, and it made her feel better just to look at him. She was sure to be mortified later because he’d caught her looking like this, but it was worth it to set eyes on the only truly welcome sight she’d seen all day.

And he'd brought one of Miss Ed's chocolate pies. She'd do just about anything to have one of those. "The door's not locked. Just bring it in and put it wherever you want while I get cleaned up. And thanks, Hoyt."

Adding that last triggered such a wave of intense feelings that Eadie was suddenly close to tears. She was worn-out and discouraged, and the man who was the biggest pleasure—and also the biggest torment—of her life had brought her supper and a chocolate pie. That not only made him the perfect end to a rotten day, but also the unexpected prize for surviving it.

Hoyt grumped something she didn't catch, then stalked away to go around to the front of the house. Eadie let the door close, then turned to open the door into the kitchen and go up the back stairs for a shower.

CHAPTER FOUR

EADIE shampooed first, then took care of the rest before she stepped out, wrapped her hair in a towel and dried off. She slipped into her bedroom for underwear, but once she put on that much, she hated the idea of getting dressed again though she had to because of Hoyt. She didn't bother with boots or shoes, opting instead for a clean pair of white socks.

Eadie didn't want to bother drying her hair either, but she forced herself to do that, too. She'd never liked going to bed with damp hair, and now that she was clean and would soon have something to eat, she'd be lucky not to fall asleep at the table, so it was just best to get this out of the way.

While she did, her nitwit heart imagined a half dozen reasons for Hoyt to have come here tonight. Not a single one had any basis in reality. As worn-out as she was, Eadie shouldn't have cared about anything more than getting something to eat before she went to sleep, but Hoyt was here, and that was so rare and special that she worried she wouldn't be able to stay awake.

By the time she went back downstairs, Eadie was almost dazed with fatigue. She hoped that eating would raise her blood sugar so she'd feel more human, because she usually did get a second wind after a good meal.

Hoyt had found enough tableware to set the kitchen table, but the covered plates were obviously from Miss Ed's kitchen. And there was a napkin-lined basket with a fat loaf of homemade bread. Hoyt had gotten out the pitcher of cold water from the refrigerator, and found glasses that he'd added ice cubes to. A stainless-steel coffee carafe that he'd also brought with him sat next to the pitcher. He was just putting cups on the table when he glanced up and saw her.

"Well," he said as he looked her over from head to sock-covered toes. "You look like a new woman." Now he offered a smile and Eadie's heart lifted a little more. "Better sit down and eat."

Eadie went to the chair he'd pulled out

for her and allowed him to seat her before she reached for the cloth napkin he'd also brought along. ''Hoyt, you can't possibly know how much this means to me tonight,'' she said. ''I'm starved.''

''Dive right in, then,'' he said as he gallantly whisked away the insulated cover from her plate to reveal a thick, gorgeous steak, a huge ladle of steamed vegetables that were piping hot, and a fat baked potato. ''I ran the plates through your microwave. I remembered to take the metal covers off first.''

''Good,'' she said, then watched as he reached for a container of sour cream and a spoon, then dug out a big dollop to hold it over her baked potato.

''Too much? Not enough?''

''Perfect,'' Eadie declared, ''and thanks. Now sit down and enjoy your own food.'' She smiled a little when he obediently went around to the other side of the table and sat down. ''How's your side, by the way?''

''This is *your* night for TLC,'' he declared, and Eadie saw traces of a proud smile as he dropped a napkin to his lap and reached for his knife and fork to start eating. He was very pleased with himself apparently, and she felt a strong nudge of affection as she cut into her steak and had a first bite. Her taste buds celebrated.

"Oh," she said around the succulent piece of beef, "this tastes...so... wonderful."

Hoyt grinned over at her. "Fill up and enjoy."

"Thanks a million, and thank Miss Ed, too," she said hastily after she finished that bite and got another. "I don't know what this is about, but I think you just might have rubbed the magic lamp." She wolfed down that next bite and got another.

Hoyt chuckled. "What?"

"Mmm...maybe the wrong analogy...or is that a metaphor?" She gave her fork a little wave and speared some vegetables, too ravenous now to talk. "Tell you later."

Eadie didn't care that she practically shoveled the food in, and miracle of miracles, by the time she inelegantly sopped up the last of the steak drippings from her plate with a chunk of the homemade bread Hoyt had cut for her, she was actually almost full.

Hoyt had graciously poured coffee for

them both, so Eadie reached for her cup and sat back to take a big sip.

"Oh, this's so good, too," she said. "It's all good—wonderful. I get so tired of my own cooking."

"You've still got the pie."

Eadie perked up again and grinned. "Oh, let's don't forget that. I feel like it's my birthday or a holiday." She thought of something then. "But wait. I asked you how your side was doing, and you never answered."

"Doing good."

"So you slept well last night," she guessed. "You're taking the antibiotic aren't you?"

"Yup. Don't want the other, though. Aspirin's fine."

Eadie nodded. "Good. How did you get cut like that, by the way? I never did hear."

Now Hoyt's smile faded a little and she sensed he didn't consider the reason for his injury a particularly stellar moment.

"Just a lucky wreck. The colt I was riding dumped me. An old piece of corrugated tin roof had blown in from somewhere and was lying along the highway fence just out of easy sight. The colt decided I needed to know it was there before someone got hurt.''

Eadie giggled at that, and it was typical of Hoyt to tell a story that way. He was grinning over at her, and she thought he was the most handsome man on planet earth. Her heart began another slow, bitter-sweet fall toward heartbreak. It would have been so much better for her to have been born someplace else, someplace so far away from Hoyt that they might never have met.

She had to break the quiet mood that had suddenly fallen between them as they stared at each other, so she made a quick try for it.

''Are you serving the pie, too, or can I do it?''

Hoyt scraped back his chair. ''I'll do the honors.''

He got up and with her directions, found the pie cutter in a drawer and dessert plates in the cupboard before he took the pie out of the refrigerator and brought it to the table. It was entertaining to watch him wield the pie cutter, then use it to try to switch an intact wedge of the pudding pie and its whipped cream topping from the glass pan to one of the plates. He managed it just barely, then set it in front of her before he did the same for himself, though with quite a bit less fuss.

"Eat all you want," he said as he sat down. "Any left over, you can keep for tomorrow."

The pie was wonderful, but by the time Eadie finished her piece, she was stuffed. A refill on her coffee finished off everything nicely.

She felt worlds better, and realized a good share of her fatigue had been because she'd pushed too hard and too long without making herself come to the house for something to eat to keep her energy up. Though she was still tired, she'd got enough of a second wind to stay awake for as long as Hoyt was here.

And why was he here anyway? Why had he brought over a delicious hot meal, then served it to her? If he was paying her back for her help yesterday and last night, he'd more than done that, and he'd been far more cheerfully accommodating than she'd been with him. And yet Eadie sensed something more, and it was difficult to keep her curiosity to herself.

"Thanks so much again, Hoyt," she said as she let him top off her coffee cup with more of the strong brew, hoping that might somehow prompt him to say something that would explain this.

"Your eyes got their sparkle back," he pointed out, and Eadie smiled a little, because he'd said it as if he was taking complete responsibility for it. He had done it, though. He could do it for her anytime by just walking into the room.

Now he gave her a narrow look. "You said you'd explain how I'd 'rubbed the magic lamp.'"

Eadie's smile shrank a little. "I also said I probably used the wrong analogy."

He gave her a grin. "But I got what you meant, and I've heard about those genies. Does feeding you tonight mean you'll grant me three wishes?"

If Eadie didn't know better, she'd think Hoyt was flirting with her. And talk about eyes that sparkled. His dark eyes had an up-to-something sparkle that was both intriguing and faintly threatening, and she felt it deep down in a way she only associated with the feminine feelings she too often had when she got close to him. Like last night.

"Do you want three wishes?"

"I've been thinking about them all through supper," he said, and there was no way to miss the sexy rasp that had come into his low voice.

Eadie knew she needed to make light of this, though there was something about him suddenly that made her feel caught. As if he somehow held her in a close grip, though he was sitting across the table from her and they weren't even close to touching. She made herself smile.

"So...what would your wishes be? And with only three, you'd have to be careful what you pick. A lady rancher with a small spread and a broke down tractor can only fulfill so many wishes at a time."

"Your tractor's broke down, huh?"

"First time this week, though," she said, not comfortable that he seemed to be a little too alert to that. "It's not a regular week if it doesn't call in sick at least one day."

She'd not meant for her mention of the tractor to be anything more than a joke about wishing for grand things, though she shouldn't have done it. They both knew she was no genie. Maybe she was still more tired than she realized and the incautious remark had slipped out because the tractor had been so on her mind. The last thing she wanted was for Hoyt to think she was hinting to him that she needed help. Or money.

She needed to move them past it. "So, tell me your wishes. I owe you something really wonderful for bringing supper tonight anyway."

"That made you happy, huh?"

"Yes, very happy. And the service was wonderful. I think you'll get a big tip."

"Maybe we could mix that big tip and those three wishes together and work out a business deal," he said.

Eadie had seen that cagey look in Hoyt's dark eyes before, usually when he was negotiating business over the phone. In another century, he might have been a horse trader or a riverboat gambler. Or a con man. Hoyt seemed to have some of the abilities, but too many scruples and far too much straightforward bluntness and love for hard work to use them to cheat anyone.

She'd admired that about him, so she wasn't worried about being cheated, though she was cautious. Something new was going on between them and she hadn't figured it out yet. Eadie tried to sound casual, though she suddenly felt anything but. Her instinct was to play dense.

"What kind of business deal? I don't think I could work any more afternoons a week for you, but I could try."

Hoyt's smile eased a little. "Not work per se, Eadie. Something personal."

Now his smile faded completely though his dark gaze was steady on her.

"I'll be thirty-four in a couple months. Past time to settle down and start a family. If something happened to me now, everything I own would go to an Eastern cousin or two I've never seen more than once. I doubt they'd be interested in taking over things. They wouldn't have the first idea how to anyway, so everything I've worked for, and everything my daddy and his daddy worked for, and his daddy before that, would be gone."

Hoyt paused a moment, as if he'd sensed her sudden discomfort, but then he went on. "I thought about it when I was sailing through the air yesterday and saw that glint of metal below. Been thinkin' about it ever since.''

He'd decided to marry. The thought came to her as strongly as if he'd spoken it out loud.

Eadie was terrified of what Hoyt might see in her eyes, so she looked down at her coffee cup and pulled it closer to tip it a little and stare into the rich brew.

As hard as it had been to know about Hoyt's girlfriends, as conflicted as she'd been about being involved with the selection of his ''parting gifts'' for the women he'd broken up with, Eadie suddenly knew she'd rather face a million of those than to hear him say that he was planning to marry and settle down.

She'd never thought about Hoyt getting married because he'd not shown a speck of interest in the idea. He wouldn't be the first bachelor who'd go to his grave unmarried.

Eadie thought about the beautiful Celeste and the fact that Hoyt's visitor that day had been a woman. If he'd been worried about what would happen to Donovan Ranch and it had been Celeste who'd come to see him today, the woman had certainly shown up at the right time and maybe put the thought of marriage in his head. Considering Hoyt's thoughts about his mortality, perhaps he'd called Celeste to come to Donovan Ranch because he'd been the one to think about marriage first.

It took Eadie a moment to realize why Hoyt might involve her in a plan to marry, if he was. It could very well be that he'd decided on Celeste, but needed some sort of help from Eadie to win her back. After all, as she understood it, Celeste had broken up with him, not the other way around, though Eadie couldn't imagine what she could do to help him.

"Did I make you uncomfortable with my mention of death?" he asked soberly.

Eadie glanced over at him, then away and smiled a little to throw him off before she scooted back her chair to stand. She had to have something to do, and began to clear the table so she could wash Miss Ed's things for the trip home. She gave Hoyt an answer to keep him from pursuing this.

"I appreciate that you realize you can't count on living forever, but if you're asking in a roundabout way if I think you should marry, then my answer is yes, go ahead. You've had any number of girlfriends who'd be happy to marry you and provide you with Donovan heirs. Either choose one of them or go out and find the one you want.''

Eadie made herself meet his dark gaze and smiled again, both to lighten things up and to keep Hoyt from guessing that her heart was suddenly cracking from the force of the hurt that was crushing it.

''I'll bet it wouldn't take you a week to find a wife. Deciding to do something is half the battle, isn't it?''

Hoyt's gaze was pushing into hers. ''Maybe.''

Eadie's nerves were starting to scream from the pressure of her worry about what might show on her face. She'd practiced a lot of years keeping her feelings to herself, and she'd had total success. She hoped for that same total success now, because Hoyt's talk of marriage was the acid test.

''S-so, what kind of business deal did you have in mind? I assume it's related to your decision to marry, though I can't imagine how. You've put me in charge of calling florists or going to the jewelers to pick out something you could put a note with and mail.''

Eadie made her smile slant with faked regret. "But those were for girlfriends. If you want me to help with things for a wife, then I'd have to tell you you're on your own from the get-go."

Relieved she'd sounded so cool about it, Eadie turned and put the things she'd gathered into the dishpan in the sink, twisted on the hot water faucet full force, then squirted in detergent. After a moment, Hoyt called over to her above the sound of the water.

"Let the dishes soak for now, Eadie."

She knew she was being a bit rude. After all, she'd refused Hoyt before he'd actually asked her to do anything. And she did owe him, so she tried to marshal just a little more of that cool, though it was almost impossible to summon. The sooner he said his piece, the sooner she could tell him no and get it over with. She turned off the tap, then turned to sit back down and give Hoyt what she hoped was a neutral look.

It had been so long since she'd seen him this serious—but not in a temper—that it somehow increased her feeling of doom. Hoyt really would marry, and soon. There was no mistaking the determination about him, and when Hoyt decided to do something, it was as good as done.

"All right," she said, and realized she was resigned to doing this one last thing for Hoyt in spite of what she'd just said. Maybe whatever it was he wanted her to do for him would kill her feelings for him, once and for all. She'd have to do that anyway once he married, because she refused to be in love, however secretly, with a married man.

"What did you have in mind?"

Hoyt smiled a little then. "The kitchen isn't the place for this, Eadie. I think I got ahead of myself."

Eadie rolled her eyes. "So you're saying 'stay tuned.' Which means I have to wait to hear this until we're someplace besides my kitchen?" She turned to face the table squarely and rested her forearms and palms on it.

"Look, Hoyt, I'm grateful for supper, but I'm tired. If you've never noticed it about me before, I'm a painfully curious person, so why don't you forget we're sitting in my kitchen and just get this over with. Then you can get home and I can go to bed."

She'd barely finished when Hoyt lifted a small black velvet box with a gold bow tied around it and set it just so between where her hands rested on the table. Eadie stared at it dumbly a moment, wondering where he'd kept it all this time, but denying with every shred of sense she had that the little black velvet box with the gold bow wasn't what it looked like. Not at all. Hoyt's low voice was a growl.

"Open it and you'll know what I want."

Eadie managed to lift her gaze from the gold bow to look over at Hoyt and search his face for any clue to this. She had to be dreaming. She'd simply gotten too sleepy, eaten too much, and in real life, she must have fallen asleep. Then she'd dreamed Hoyt's confession about realizing his mortality yesterday and deciding to find a wife. Once her love-addled brain had come up with that much, it was imagining even more wildly creative—and impossibly pitiful—fantasies that could never be.

Almost desperate to prove that she was dreaming and that the box wasn't real, Eadie gamely picked it up and slipped off the bow. But if this was a dream, then it was a doozy, because the box and the bow felt real. Eadie took that last daring step and opened the little box…

CHAPTER FIVE

THE gold ring inside had a diamond that, in the right light, was large enough to signal satellites. Eadie snapped the box closed and stood up to lean across the table and set it in front of Hoyt before she straightened.

Hoyt sat back in his chair to stare at her. He looked stunned. Well, so was she. And maybe insulted. If this was a joke, it was a rotten one she never would have expected from him.

"Your ring is beautiful," she said casually. "If you aren't sure Celeste will take you back, flash that little trinket at her." Now she made herself smile, though her lips were so stiff they ached a little. "And see? You've got great taste in jewelry after all. You could have been picking out those other little keepsakes just fine all along."

Unable to keep from feeling injured by both Hoyt's declaration that he needed to find a wife and this…this whatever it was, Eadie turned to the sink. She started washing Miss Ed's things for the trip home, giving them a quick rinse, then sitting them in the dish rack.

The silence between them stretched, along with her nerves, so when those few things were draining, she dried her hands. The wicker basket Hoyt had brought was sitting inside the pantry, so in an effort to get him out of her house as quickly as possible, she retrieved the basket and brought it over to the end of the table.

Now that she was back, Hoyt gave a dry chuckle. "You don't get it, do you?"

"Get what?" she said as she quickly dried Miss Ed's things and set them in the basket.

"*You're* the woman I want to marry, Eadie. You."

Eadie's hands stilled. Her heart began to shake with the magnitude of the longing that went through her. And the hurt. She rested a hand on the edge of the basket and gripped it, but the stiff woven wood felt as flimsy and insubstantial as she suddenly did.

Her voice was choked with the force of

the emotions that were strangling her. "Is that the business deal you wanted to make with me?"

"That's it."

Hoyt sounded pleased with himself, but Eadie couldn't look at him to see for sure.

Oh, God, she'd give anything to marry Hoyt Donovan! It was the dearest dream of her life to have him propose marriage. But the first part of that dream had been for him to finally notice her as a woman and fall in love. And to fall in love with her so completely that he forgot about the beauties.

But this was about business, not love. Hoyt was suddenly feeling his mortality and he'd gotten the urge to marry as soon as possible to sire heirs and continue the Donovan family legacy. It could very well be that the only reason he'd chosen her was because she'd been around at the right moment.

Good old Eadie Webb. She doesn't have any prospects, so why not get her to do it?

Though this was the chance of a lifetime, Eadie forced herself to cling to common sense. "H-how long would this marriage last after you had your heir?"

"The usual length of time, of course.

And I'd like to have more than one kid. Why marry at all if it's not meant to be permanent?"

Eadie looked over to see the crankiness about him, as if he was offended by her lack of enthusiasm. How dense was he anyway? She'd credited Hoyt with smarts because he really was a smart man. Far smarter than she was because his ranch was growing more successful all the time while hers was slowly failing.

But when it came to women, Hoyt was a dunce. He was a dunce about her, too, if he thought she'd be overjoyed about this.

"Oh, Hoyt," she said, unable to keep her disappointment in him out of her voice. "You haven't stayed with one woman for longer than a few weeks. It takes nine months for a baby to arrive."

That rubbed him wrong, and his expression suddenly went stormy. "So you think I couldn't stay faithful?"

"You…lose interest. Too fast."

"Marriage isn't about staying interested, it's about commitment."

"Yes it is about commitment," she said. "But it needs to be more."

"You don't think we care about each other enough to make it more?"

"I don't know," she said candidly then shrugged. "Actually, what you're really looking for is a brood mare."

The silence that suddenly fell between them carried the punch of a thunderclap.

"A wha-ha-hat?" Hoyt's disbelieving chuckle wasn't at all amused.

"A brood mare."

Hoyt looked away, annoyed. It was his *Ah, hell, Eadie,* look. His dark gaze came back to hers and she saw the snap of temper in it.

"I *am not* looking for a brood mare, Eadie." His gaze narrowed a little, as if he'd just thought of something. "But even though *I'm* not, *you* were all for the 'brood mare' idea when it was Celeste or some other woman. Now you're going prickly."

"Well, duh," she said flatly.

Hoyt's anger abruptly cooled into an almost-grin as he got the point, but he fought it to make an effort to look earnest.

"You know I'm a man of my word, Eadie. If I marry you, we stay married till you plant me in the ground." He paused then, and warmed to his subject. The moment he started up again, Eadie knew he would try to close the "deal."

"I see it this way," Hoyt went on. "You don't have much family, neither do I. So we make our own family, have babies. I already trust you with everything I own, and I think you trust me. You and I get along…in our way. You've seen me at my worst and not run screamin' for the road, and I've seen you at your worst, like now when you're going balky on me again. But time's movin' on for us both. I say we just grab onto this and see where it goes."

Eadie nodded almost absently as she stared at Hoyt's ruggedly handsome face, still a little in shock over this. The storm clouds had passed and now that he'd laid out what he must think was his best argument, he looked hopeful.

But when she didn't comment right away, a hint of somberness came over him, and after a few quiet moments, his voice lowered to a gravelly rasp.

"You know I'd never hurt you, Eadie."

It was a reference to that night. Eadie felt her heart squeeze, and she gave him a sad smile. "I know, Hoyt."

"I'm hoping...that night showed you how I...am."

The power of what Eadie felt for him suddenly made it difficult to stay dry-eyed, but once she could get control of herself, her voice was too choked to speak above a bare whisper.

"I know."

"You aren't worried about that, are you?" he asked gently, and her eyes began to sting with love. "Because if you are, I wish you wouldn't worry." He looked away a little. "Things between a man and a woman were meant to be good. Tender."

Eadie knew Hoyt had never quite believed she hadn't been raped, in spite of her insistence that her date hadn't got that far before she'd fought him off and escaped. What Hoyt was saying now was a clear indication of his misbelief. But he wanted to marry her anyway, and was trying to let her know he was prepared to be patient with her, and to be gentle.

He looked at her again and as much as said so. "I'd be careful with you, Eadie. Always. You know that, don't you?"

Oh, he was trying so hard! And he meant

it. She'd never known Hoyt to break his word.

"I know."

Her voice cracked on that, and his dear, familiar face began to blur. Hoyt cleared his throat, as if he was too macho to be completely comfortable with a glimpse of tears.

He'd been that way five years ago when she'd broken down in his arms. She'd been sobbing. But he'd held her and said all the kind, soothing words any woman would have wanted to hear, so she absolutely knew his discomfort was because he couldn't tolerate the hurt behind the tears, not because he felt any true impatience or scorn for the tears themselves.

"Besides," he said gruffly, "going through with this might be the only way either of us would ever marry, right?"

It was typical Hoyt Donovan logic, and she couldn't exactly refute it. Eadie bit her lips to somehow get control of the wildly surging ocean of hot tears that were about to burst up in twin geysers.

Oh, how she loved this big, blunt, grumpy, *thickheaded,* blustery cowboy, and she would forever. So why was she even pretending she could withstand his crazy idea about marrying her?

"I'll marry you."

Eadie hadn't consciously put those hoarse words together; they'd just gusted out on a pent-up breath. It took her a moment to recover from hearing herself say them, so she made sure her next words would help conceal the fierce love that had driven the first ones out.

"But if you ever get over feeling mortal, I think I can find a way to remind you."

Hoyt burst out with a roaring laugh that signaled his delight with that—and his delight that she wasn't going to cry.

"Spoken like the only lady in Texas who could handle me," he declared, then laughed again as if he was proud of it.

And maybe proud of her. Eadie knew he enjoyed her prickliness almost as much as he enjoyed complaining about it.

"Oh, Eadie, come on over here," he said as his laughter wound down. He scraped his chair back from the table and slapped his hands on his thighs. "Come on, darlin'. We'd best take care of that ring."

Eadie took the two steps between them, then stopped when it dawned on her that he meant for her to sit on his lap. He caught her hand anyway and in an instant she was doing just that. Eadie couldn't help that she went stiff with self-consciousness as she sat across his thighs with his arm around her waist.

His thighs and arm felt hard and strong and the heat from them and the rest of Hoyt's big body went around and through her like a flame through paper. Hoyt reached for the velvet box and took out the beautiful ring.

"Let's see that little ring finger, see if I guessed this right," he said, and Eadie couldn't miss the pleasure he seemed to take as he singled out her finger and slipped the ring into place. He lifted her hand to give them both a good view of the way the beautiful ring looked.

"Looks perfect to me, how's it feel?" he asked, and Eadie could hardly tear her gaze away from his happy, relaxed smile to look.

"It's perfect, Hoyt. And beautiful," she added, so unable to fully grasp this that she stared dumbly at the ring. Hoyt tightened his fingers around hers and lowered her hand.

"Hey there, pretty gal."

Eadie automatically turned her head to look into Hoyt's face when he said that, but instead found her lips caught by his.

Years of wondering what Hoyt's lips might feel like on hers hadn't prepared her for the real thing. His lips were firm and warm, almost hot, but they were expert, devastatingly expert. There was a leashed passion behind them but they were gentle, and as they moved over hers to coax and caress, Eadie felt every bone in her body melt. Hoyt's low growl was a playful sound of male hunger that sent sparkling shards of pleasure through her and impacted her most feminine places.

Hoyt growled again, and she felt the warm lick of his tongue against her lips before he gently pushed past the soft barrier. Eadie's arms had somehow gone around his neck and it was she who pressed closer for more, more of this.

If Hoyt hadn't reasserted his natural dominance and begun to slowly bring the kiss to an end, Eadie might have fainted from the stark pleasure of what his lips, and at the last, what his hands had been doing to her. She'd not felt so much as a wisp of fear, much less self-consciousness, because the naturalness of this between them, the *rightness* of it, had been a constant pulse in her heart.

The dizzying idea that Hoyt wanted to marry her—and just then she didn't care *why* he wanted to, only that he did—sent a nettle of panic through her. What if he changed his mind?

All of this had been so spur of the moment, so sudden, with no foundation at all except his sudden sense of mortality. What if Hoyt had second thoughts tomorrow? What if he changed his mind on some other sudden whim?

Hoyt's voice was rough, as if he wasn't quite as in control as he seemed to be. "Have you got a big objection to getting hitched tomorrow? Or are you one who's always wanted a big wedding with a few hundred guests?"

He drew back a little and Eadie, though her head was still swimming, was able to focus on his smiling mouth. "'Cause I think we just lit a very short fuse." He took a moment to give her another kiss. "That doesn't...overwhelm you, does it?"

Eadie gave her head a small dazed shake.

"Is that a 'No, Hoyt, I'm not overwhelmed by that kiss,' or is that a 'No, Hoyt, tomorrow's too soon, I want the white wedding?'"

"I'm not...overwhelmed."

"Good," he said as he pressed a kiss to her forehead. "You know all you'd ever need to do is tell me no, don't you?"

Her quiet, "I know," was soft again with emotion.

He drew back a little. "You know lots of things about me, don't you?"

Eadie looked into his eyes and smiled. "A few."

Hoyt's voice dropped to a gravelly whisper. "Then you know how bad I want to do this tomorrow? How I'd just as soon take you to Las Vegas?"

"There's no middle ground between tomorrow and something a few weeks or months away?" she ventured, and yet the part of her that wanted this—wanted him—was afraid to give him time to change his mind.

"Are you scared?" he asked.

"I'd be an idiot if I wasn't."

He grinned. "Ah, we'll do fine, Eadie, you'll see."

"How about a week from tomorrow?" Eadie watched his face to see how he took that, because he looked anything but nervous about getting married. That was unusual for such a long-time bachelor. And yet Eadie knew if he was nervous, Hoyt would eat dirt and die before he'd let on.

"I reckon that might be okay," he said as he appeared to consider it. "Get a preacher for private vows in the parlor at Donovan about midafternoon, then celebrate with a barbecue for everyone we know, and a dance when the sun goes down."

Eadie tried not to wince at the amount of work that would entail. And to do it all in a week's time was impossible. Hoyt would never think about the mechanics though. When it came to celebrations on Donovan Ranch, he tended to order up barbecues and dances on an enormous scale, and he rarely contributed more than a hazy list of what he wanted and the money. So to him, those kind of things appeared to come together like magic.

"Don't you think that would be too much for Miss Ed on such short notice?" she asked.

"Maybe," he allowed as his eyes narrowed playfully and he studied her flushed face. Eadie couldn't get over how excited he seemed to be about this. And eager. "You're a little too balky, so let's start over. How 'bout private vows in the church chapel next Saturday afternoon? Closest friends only?"

That much was doable. "All right."

"But I want you to have the white dress, Eadie, fancy as you want, and as many flowers as you can stand. I'll wear a tux. And we'll get a photograph of us, more than one. I'll ask Miss Ed tomorrow what she might want to do about a celebration at Donovan, and let her pick what she wants to do. Maybe she'd want to do it in a couple weeks or so, but I want you to pick the honeymoon to go on right away so I can set that up. You say where, and money's no object."

As usual, Hoyt tended more toward generosity than thrift. And he had employees who could take up the slack during his absence, so he needed to be reminded about her less flexible situation.

"Oh, Hoyt," she cautioned gently. "I can't just up and leave my place."

"Well, I want a honeymoon," he declared, and Eadie wondered if she'd ever seen him so happy and enthusiastic. "So how 'bout before the fall gather? You'd have time to get squared away, make the business decisions you want. Would that solve it for you?"

"Yes."

"Good," he said, then grinned and lowered his voice to a confidential tone. "Are you noticing how easy I am to get along with all of a sudden? How I throw something out and you throw something back, and I knuckle under like a meek little lamb?"

Eadie was the one who laughed then. Hoyt hugged her close and she was filled with such joy and hope—and terror—that she didn't know if she could keep from lapsing into tears.

That next week was an even more potent mix of that same joy, hope and terror. After the weekend, Eadie began to feel a little less leery of Hoyt changing his mind, so after they went to the courthouse on Monday morning to get the marriage license, she took the rest of the day to find a wedding dress. She tried not to think about the fact that the cost of it took her last good credit card to its limit.

She raced to keep up with her work at home and do her part with the plans Miss Ed had agreed to, but she'd also had to start moving a few of her things to Donovan Ranch. Since they were all busy, the only time she got to spend alone with Hoyt was in the evenings, but he'd kept that time short. It was clear he was determined to keep the physical side of their engagement to a minimum.

And so chaste that they were almost back to the usual level of boss and employee. A couple of brief kisses and warm hugs were nothing remotely like that kiss the other night, but as Saturday approached Eadie began to worry about their wedding night.

Her worries weren't because of what had happened that night five years ago, because it had only gone so far, but because everything about Hoyt's sudden proposal and his headlong rush to the ceremony made her want to wait for the most intimate part. Since there'd been a lack of physical contact between them that week, she was worried that everything would abruptly change on their wedding night because lovemaking was expected. She'd hoped for the physical part of their relationship to have some sort of escalation, but that wasn't happening.

Besides, what she really wanted before full intimacy was to hear Hoyt say he loved her, though she didn't only want him to say the words, she wanted them to be true. The last thing she wanted was for him to feel compelled to say them because she was his wife. Eadie didn't doubt that Hoyt cared for her, but he'd made the decision to marry so suddenly that there couldn't have been time enough for him to fall in love.

It was even possible that he never truly would. As far as she knew, Hoyt had never been in love before, though he'd certainly given himself opportunity after opportunity with scores of other women.

Meanwhile, Hoyt had become so magnanimous and accommodating in every other way that it was a big adjustment. Even Miss Ed had remarked on it one afternoon when Eadie had been at Donovan Ranch.

"Have you seen the boss anywhere the past few days?" Miss Ed had asked, then given her head a shake. "'Cause if he don't show up soon, I believe we'll have to call the sheriff and file a missing person's report."

She and Eadie had laughed over that, but they were both thrilled that Hoyt seemed relaxed and happy in a way he hadn't been for years. It was hard for Eadie not to feel flattered by that, because the only thing that was different in Hoyt's life to bring about that change was the fact that he was marrying her on Saturday. And yet Eadie was wary that his happy, relaxed mood might somehow give him the idea that he was in love when he might not be.

Surely not though, considering those cool, very chaste few kisses. She'd never heard Hoyt use the word love in any context, so he may not even think in terms of love no matter what he thought a wife would want to hear.

In the end, Eadie had to stop worrying about that because last minute details took all her attention. And then the moment came when she was walking up the aisle in the blossom choked chapel of the small country church. Miss Ed and several of their closest friends were present to witness the modest ceremony, and the time for second thoughts was gone.

CHAPTER SIX

HOYT was so ruggedly handsome in his black tuxedo that Eadie ached when she saw him. But the moment he'd fully turned to watch her approach the place at the front where he and the pastor waited, she knew he was edgy.

He'd been a rock the whole week, behaving as if he hadn't a care in the world, but now his rugged face was stony and before Eadie was halfway up the aisle, she saw the restlessness about him. Though her white veil cast the chapel in a pristine haze, she sensed it as much as saw it through the fine net.

So the magnitude of what Hoyt was doing with her today had finally struck him, and now that it had, Eadie suddenly had such a sharp attack of nerves that she felt faint. Oh, Lord, what if he changed his mind here?

The moment that thought came, another

thought—equally hysterical—followed to counter it. Hoyt's best friend, Reece Waverly, was standing by with his wife, Leah, and son, Bobby, and Reece would surely chase him down and bring him back if he tried to duck out. Though Eadie knew it was a wild scenario, very little about all this wasn't wild or out of the ordinary.

It pleased her though that Reece had made no secret of the fact that he heartily approved of this marriage. His wife, Leah, was someone Eadie didn't know well yet, but figured she soon would. And Leah was so hugely pregnant and radiant that, more than once, Eadie found her gaze straying to her.

One of Eadie's dearest friends, Corrie Davis Merrick, was also among the group of their friends, along with her new husband, Nick. Corrie had married Nick a few months ago, and she was not only blissfully happy, but two months pregnant.

The fact that Eadie suddenly noticed two more obviously pregnant women among Hoyt's married friends as she walked up the aisle made her wonder if having so many pregnant women around would make Hoyt even more eager to add to the crop of babies in their part of Texas. If so, he probably wouldn't be thrilled that she preferred to wait until she was sure they'd gotten their marriage off to a solid start. At least his craving for babies might well be the thing that would keep him from bolting now.

When Eadie reached Hoyt's side, he took her hand and she felt reassured by his strong, gentle grip. As he smiled down at her, she felt him relax.

The pastor led them in the vows. Hoyt relaxed even more then and spoke in the right places. There was no hint of hesitation or lack of confidence in his "I do's," so Eadie tried for the same in her responses. When it came time to put the wedding ring on her finger, Hoyt slid it silently onto her finger.

"I now pronounce you husband and wife," the pastor declared. "You may now kiss your bride, Mr. Donovan."

Hoyt managed the fragile veil deftly, then slid his arms around her and bent down.

His growling, "I thought we'd never get to this part," preceded a tender but thorough kiss that made Eadie think his plans for tonight would be quite traditional. When he drew back, the minister introduced them as Mr. and Mrs. Hoyt Donovan, and their friends and Miss Ed applauded.

Afterward, the San Antonio photographer Hoyt had flown in took dozens of photos, both inside and outside the chapel and church. At Hoyt's insistence, their friends were also photographed, and he finally coaxed Miss Ed to pose. Eadie would be throwing her bouquet later for the reception guests at the house, so Hoyt escorted her through a light hail of birdseed to his SUV, which had been decorated by his friends.

The big vehicle sported Just Married signs and streamers, with a rope of tin cans and old boots tied to the back bumper to trail them down the road. The inside was scattered with birdseed and crammed with so many balloons that Hoyt had to break several to make room for them in the front seat.

By the time they pulled out of the parking lot of the old church and took off down the highway to Donovan Ranch with a line of other vehicles behind them, Eadie was flushed with relief and amusement. Hoyt had leaned over to give her a quick kiss before he'd started the engine, then he'd immediately reached up to run a finger around the inside of his shirt collar after he'd drawn back. She could see the sparkle of perspiration at his temples and knew it wasn't from the heat, but rather from some form of delayed reaction.

Hoyt had seemed relaxed this week and happy, tense only before the ceremony began, but there was an uncommon somberness about him now. Almost as if he was a little in shock, and Eadie wasn't sure what to do about it. She suddenly felt a hefty share of the same somber shock, and her amusement fled.

They'd certainly jumped into this marriage far too fast, but she did think that what Hoyt had said the other night was true: neither of them might ever have married unless they'd done it this way, at least not to each other. And maybe Eadie never would have married, because for her, no man compared with Hoyt. It might be just as true that Hoyt would never have gone through with this if he'd waited longer than a week to do it.

She and Hoyt at least had the benefit of

long acquaintance, and there was love between them if only on her side. She believed Hoyt truly did care for her and trusted her, so she had at least a reasonable hope that what he felt for her might one day grow into at least a little more.

Eadie looked down at her beautiful rings a moment, then closed her eyes to make a silent, fervent prayer that she and Hoyt really would have a family together, a loving one. The extra part of Eadie's prayer was that Hoyt would also someday come to love her.

By the time they got to the Donovan Ranch house, both sides of the long driveway, most of the front lawn and all of the lanes around the big headquarters were cluttered with cars and pickups and SUVs. Eadie was shocked at the number of people who'd turned out on such short notice, though they'd been expecting a large crowd. That was also why Miss Ed had hired extra help for the day.

Eadie certainly didn't know a lot of these people, and from some of the license plates she spied here and there, several had come from other parts of Texas. There were even a couple rental cars. She'd known at least three people were flying in for the reception and open house. Since the airstrip was a mile behind the house, it wasn't visible from the ranch road, so Eadie couldn't tell if any of them had arrived yet.

Miss Ed had insisted on a cake and champagne reception and an open house that included a catered cold buffet supper later on. There'd be no country band and no dancing, so the huge house was certain to be wall-to-wall well-wishers, though the big patio and grounds out back were shady and would no doubt attract many of their guests.

Hoyt had managed to get a lot of the things he'd initially wanted that Eadie had considered impossible on such short notice. It was probably because he was not only a can-do sort of man, but a lot of people snapped to when he gave an order.

Hoyt drove them right up on the lawn and stopped the SUV so it was positioned across the wide front walk. He was out in a flash, then came around to her side to open the door and help her out. Eadie tried to keep her trailing veil corralled, but there was enough of a breeze to tease some of its folds out of her grip.

As she caught them, Eadie spied Mike and Mose in the side yard chasing a handful of small boys, who were running in circles. She should have known Hoyt would encourage parents to bring their kids.

"Did I tell you how beautiful you are today, Miss Eadie?" Hoyt said before he leaned close and his warm breath gusted across her ear. "And that dress makes you look like the Good Fairy. I think I'm gonna pay every kid a dollar for any one of those little pearls that might fall off. I wouldn't want to lose a speck of your magic."

It was a playfully romantic thing to say, and Eadie's heart was struck hard by it. "Any magic I have belongs to my husband," she whispered back, careful to keep her voice down because several guests were swarming out the front double doors of the big house.

Hoyt's lips brushed her cheek and before she realized what he would do, he swept her up in his arms, then backed up a step to kick the door closed before he turned to carry her to the house. If his side was still bothering him, there was no hint of it now. The small crowd showered them with more birdseed before Hoyt got her over the threshold and into the wide stone foyer. He carried her on through the house to the dining room where Miss Ed waited with the multitier wedding cake that was flanked by two enormous sheet cakes.

Hoyt set her on her feet, helped her readjust the veil so it trailed out of the way down her back, then they observed the usual tradition with the wedding cake, cutting a small piece to feed to each other. Eadie was pleased that Hoyt politely fed her a bit of cake, instead of making a mess of it as she'd seen other brides and grooms do to each other. It always stole a little of her respect for a couple and her optimism for their future to see that kind of thing, because it seemed so immature and disrespectful.

She was thrilled to know that as much of a rounder as Hoyt had been in the past, he behaved with nothing but respect and regard for her. It was her delight to feed a bit of cake to him, even more so when he caught her wrist and his lips nibbled a little at her fingers—with the vocal approval of their guests—before he lowered her hand.

Hoyt opened the first bottle of champagne and they drank a toast to each other before everyone else joined them for both cake and champagne. While their guests started through the lines that moved along both sides of the table, Hoyt led her out and through the congested hall into the big living room, where Miss Ed had ordered two of the high-backed chairs from the dining room to be set on the sheet-covered hearth in front of the massive stone fireplace. Eadie took off her veil to drape it over a chair back. Hoyt sat down next to her as the first of their guests came by to express their congratulations and best wishes.

It was a wonderful day, a spectacular one, and Eadie's heart began to lose track of her worries. Not too long after that, she caught sight of one of Hoyt's old girlfriends in the line of friends and neighbors and Donovan ranch employees who moved steadily past them.

This was obviously another result of the full-page wedding announcement Hoyt had put in the newspaper that week. Eadie had been appalled at the public invitation to their open house, which Hoyt had directed to "Friends, Employees and Business Associates of Miss Eadie Webb and Mr. Hoyt Donovan," but she'd not let Hoyt know that because he'd been so pleased with his idea.

Eadie had successfully hidden her horror over the newspaper invitation, but it was suddenly impossible to hide her mirth as the occasional ex-girlfriend made her way through the line and came past to wish them well.

Eadie pleasantly accepted their polite but slightly insincere best wishes to her, but the hardest part was keeping her amusement to herself when she recognized several of the pieces of jewelry she'd picked out at one time or another. It seemed to be an ex-girlfriend conspiracy and the occasional look of consternation on Hoyt's face was priceless, because he'd apparently noticed that they were wearing his "parting gifts," as if each were sending some sort of secret message.

It relieved Eadie that Hoyt managed to find a half dozen successful ways to avoid good luck kisses from each of them, but she was mightily impressed when he quelled the intentions of one persistent brunette by adding his legendary glare when she leaned close. The brunette froze just short of the big kiss she'd been about to land on his lean cheek, but then she abruptly straightened with the kiss undelivered.

After the brunette stalked away, Eadie leaned over to whisper a discreet, "I saw that," to Hoyt. Though he was still out of sorts over the near kiss, he flashed Eadie a look that was a bit sheepish.

"I thought you were going to have to save me from one of the bigger errors of my bachelor days," he growled then grinned. "So how am I doin' as a faithful husband?"

Tickled by his playful mood Eadie whispered back a slightly tepid, "Passable."

There wasn't a speck of seriousness or regret about Hoyt now over what they'd done that day, and Eadie felt secure enough to tease him a little more.

"And did you notice some of the jewelry they were wearing? I think I saw every one of those exact same pieces at Rhodes' Jewelers."

Hoyt frowned over that. "Looked familiar to me, too."

After the next guest moved past, Hoyt leaned closer to say, "I apologize, Eadie."

Eadie's gaze met his and she saw the twinkle there as he went on.

"But since they all paraded them by like little trophies, I hope that proves what a prize you got for a husband." A badly suppressed smile broke free as some of his macho ego seeped through. "I'm all yours now, though, including my account at Rhodes'. Till that day I mentioned the other night."

Eadie recalled that Hoyt had said he'd stay married to her until she planted him in the ground.

Her brisk, "Let's hope today isn't that day," made him burst out with a laugh then squeeze her hand and lean close to give her a brief, hard kiss.

"I'll behave myself, Eadie Reginie," he whispered, "just see if I don't," before he drew back to greet the next person in the line of guests that kept drifting by.

Eadie Reginie.

No one had ever called her that, but the fun way Hoyt had said the name gave Eadie a warm feeling, and she loved the cheeriness in it. Hoyt seemed to be having a good time holding court with her, and she couldn't help feeling sentimental over that.

Hoyt was such a big, blatantly masculine and macho male who was so often given to grumpiness and temper, that the contrast between grouse and playful kid was strongly appealing to her. But of course nearly everything Hoyt did appealed to her, since there wasn't a speck of meanness or cruelty in him, despite his sometimes volatile temper.

After most of their guests had come past and they began to see several others carrying plates of the cold sandwiches and finger foods from the big tables set up in the huge ranch kitchen, they got up to mingle their way through the house.

That's when they encountered most of the children who'd come along with their families. Several, including Reece and Leah's son Bobby, had been outdoors on the patio or in the yard where a handful of teenagers had conducted games, but most of the kids had now come in for sandwiches and cake.

Some of the little boys were already on their way back outside, and Hoyt nudged Eadie to draw her attention to a small troop who had cut through the dining room to get to the kitchen and the patio doors. From the looks of it, each one had grabbed an extra piece of cake that they carried in one hand and ate as they went, occasionally dropping a glob of crumbs and frosting. At least two had mints stuffed in their shirt pockets.

Hoyt chuckled and leaned close to remark to Eadie about it when she felt a sharp tug on her dress that made her glance back.

A tiny girl in a bright pink dress, who was perhaps no older than two, had slipped close and taken a small handful of the seed pearl flowers on the skirt of her wedding dress. Eadie turned to the toddler. Hoyt moved with her to look on as the little girl pulled her hand away from the satin fabric and glanced up.

"Hello, sweetheart," Eadie said softly.

"Hey there, sugar," Hoyt added as he leaned down and gave the child a smile. "Ain't you got on a pretty pink dress? It's almost as pretty as you are today."

The child stuck her fingers in her mouth and smiled bashfully at Hoyt as if he was the most charming creature she'd ever met.

Eadie all but rolled her eyes at yet another adoring female.

"And what's that you've got in your mouth?" Hoyt asked then as he hunkered down for a closer look. The little girl obligingly pulled her fingers out of her mouth and held them toward him. Hoyt bravely took hold of those damp little fingers, and Eadie felt a giggle bubble up as Hoyt's thumb and finger came away with one of the larger pearls from her dress. And from the look of it now, a very wet pearl.

The little girl had either found it on the floor somewhere or simply pulled it off Eadie's dress just now. What Hoyt had said earlier about paying kids a dollar for every seed pearl that might come off was now more than a romantic little joke. The child started to turn away but Hoyt stopped her.

"Hey wait a minute, little sis. I've got something for you, too." Hoyt straightened enough to slip a hand in his pants pocket and pull out a dollar. The toddler took it and retreated to where her mommy and daddy had stood watching.

Eadie laughed as Hoyt straightened, the wet pearl now in his big palm.

"She did a good job washin' it off,

huh?'' he asked Eadie with a wink as he slipped the pearl in his pocket. ''And, just in case you were wondering, I'd like about a half dozen like that little one,'' he said and took a moment to again glance after the child before he looked back at Eadie. ''And at least six of the other kind.''

Eadie sobered a little. ''I don't want a dozen.''

Hoyt grinned. ''Neither do I, but I'll take however many you want to give after two of each. I wouldn't mind having a couple rascals like those boys who raided the cake and rustled all the mints.''

Eadie smiled but before she could come up with something to say, Miss Ed came rushing up and interrupted.

''Reece wanted me to pass on their thanks for the hospitality and their good-byes. Miss Leah's been having contractions since they left the church. Yesterday was her due day, you know.''

Hoyt took that in and sent Eadie a sparkling glance. ''How 'bout that? It'd be something if it was born today.''

Miss Ed's, ''Sure would,'' reclaimed his attention. ''It'll be up to the two of you now to bring the next generation of Donovans into this house.''

Hoyt grinned. ''You'd like that, huh?''

''Who wouldn't? Might be fun to see who they'd take after, you or Miss Eadie.''

And then Miss Ed rushed off. Hoyt sent Eadie a frown. ''Something tells me she kept the rest of that to herself.''

Eadie smiled. ''Oh, I'm sure she meant it in the best way.''

''And now you're covering for her.'' Hoyt's dark gaze was lit with amusement. ''I'll have you both know that I was the best behaved infant ever delivered at the Coulter City hospital.''

Eadie smiled again. ''Infant?''

''I mighta had the usual hard time afterward, stayin' well behaved, but that's just bein' a boy, Miss Eadie. Nothing out of the ordinary. Say, when are you gonna throw that bouquet?''

Eadie giggled a little at the telling change of subject. ''I should have asked Miss Ed what she thought. It would be best to do it before people start going home.''

''Where's it at?''

''Probably in the refrigerator. Why don't you go on into the living room, and I'll go check with Miss Ed?''

CHAPTER SEVEN

THE single ladies began to congregate in the big living room for the bridal bouquet tradition. The fact that several of them were Hoyt's old girlfriends amused Eadie, though she was careful not to let that show. When the dozen or so who wanted to participate were ready, Eadie turned away then tossed the bouquet over her shoulder before she glanced back to see who'd caught it.

The woman who had held the bouquet high, but another woman rudely jostled the lucky woman's arm. Someone else swung a hand to knock the bouquet away, which sent it tumbling through the air. The mad scramble to catch it was stunning to watch, and the crowd of onlookers in the big room erupted in hoots of laughter and shouts of encouragement.

Eadie had been to a lot of weddings, but she'd never seen anything quite like the small, brief brawl over her bouquet. She glanced over to see Hoyt's shocked face, but a sharp shriek drew Eadie's attention back in time to see the brunette emerge from the press of the others with the battered bouquet clutched against her in one hand and her arm up to block any challengers.

Which set off a fresh round of laughter and hoots. Eadie edged closer to Hoyt and he glared down at her. "What was that all about?" he groused.

"Maybe you should have waited to marry me until you saw how many other eager contenders were available," Eadie said.

Hoyt ignored that, still stunned. "Did you ever do something like that over a handful of taped-together flowers?"

"Never," Eadie said truthfully. "It's more fun to see who it goes to naturally."

"Well, good. Glad to hear it. But then, you've got too much horse sense to act that way." Hoyt nodded toward the slowly dispersing competitors, oblivious to the idea that Eadie wasn't exactly thrilled to be told she had horse sense, though it was high praise coming from Hoyt. "If I'd seen something like that before today, I'da high-tailed it to the highway by now.''

Hoyt ran a finger around the inside of his shirt collar, and Eadie sensed right away that it was a subconscious gesture of unease. Which was perfectly in keeping with the notion of a bachelor who'd had a lifelong habit of avoiding even the thought of marriage.

After all, tradition dictated that catching the bride's bouquet was supposed to indicate which single woman would marry next, which Hoyt seemed to know. The fact that the dozen or so single women here had all but come to blows in a wild bid to be the next woman down the aisle had to be appalling to any bachelor who'd been close by to witness it.

Eadie boldly slipped her arm through Hoyt's. ''Well, you're safely married now, boss. I'll protect you.''

Hoyt's grumpy glare came back to hers and she saw the twinkle of reluctant amusement in it.

''I'm sure I'll regret pointing it out now, Miss Eadie, but I'm not your boss anymore.''

Eadie smiled. "I'd say you're a very perceptive man."

"Do tell," he said as his dark brows went up. "You tricked me into sayin' that, didn't you?"

Eadie gave a little shrug and Hoyt put his hand over the back of hers and chuckled. And of course, the affection in that thrilled her.

It was almost nine o'clock before Miss Ed's crew finished cleaning up and putting the house back in order. Eadie and Hoyt had been having a last glass of champagne in the silent living room, and now they listened to Miss Ed's car go past the house toward the highway. The lights in the house were already off except for a single lamp in the living room.

Hoyt took her empty wine flute and set it on the table next to his before he sat back and took her hand. After a moment, his grip tightened warmly.

"Well, we did it, Miss Eadie."

Eadie looked down at their hands, nervous, excited, but tired from the long day. "Yes, we did. It hardly seems possible."

Hoyt shifted their hands, and she sensed a thread of nervousness in him. Which was amazing because she was nervous enough for them both. And Hoyt was the experienced one, so why would he be nervous? At the ceremony, yes, but surely not now. His voice was low but, as always, his words were blunt.

"Since you've got to be as tired of wearing that dress as I am of wearing this monkey suit, how 'bout we go get them off?"

Eadie looked up into his dark gaze and saw the glint of humor there as a faint smile ghosted over his handsome mouth.

"Ah, Miss Eadie. That's not as rude as it sounds. It's just that I'm thinkin' about how long it might take to unbutton all those tiny little buttons down your back. It doesn't mean I'm in a big rush to get you to myself, though I am. Why, it'll be midnight now before I get through those buttons."

He leaned toward her and his warm lips eased softly onto hers. Eadie's lashes drifted shut. For better or worse, she was Hoyt's wife. What would happen next was what needed to happen on a wedding night. And she loved Hoyt, more by the moment, so if he didn't quite love her yet, surely she could be content with this much. And she was married to him. That alone was worth the earth.

As if he sensed her tension, he drew back. ‘‘You remember what I told you the other night, don’t you? You’re the one who says how much or how little. I promised you that.’’

Eadie felt a burst of emotion that got her by the throat. ‘‘I know. But you need to know that things truly didn’t go as far that night as you always seemed to think. You never seemed to...believe me.’’

‘‘I believe you, Eadie,’’ he said softly. ‘‘You haven’t been fretting about that, have you?’’

‘‘A little.’’

‘‘Well, don’t. But for the record, that first rough touch was too far, all by itself. That will never happen between us.’’

Eadie pulled her hand from his and slid her arms around his neck to hug him close. She couldn’t have stopped herself from hugging him anyway, not after that. And she’d dreamed of doing things like this, touching him, hugging him, expressing at least some of what she felt for him. Now that she was Hoyt’s wife, she had the right to do little things, and she felt a steadily rising joy as it began to dawn on her more fully.

Hoyt's arms went around her and after a moment, he shifted to reach behind her and the single lamp in the room went off. A moment more and he moved again, only this time he drew back to slide one arm under her before he stood and lifted her with him. Eadie instantly remembered his side. "Are you sure you should be doing this again? Your stitches just came out yesterday."

"Ah, I'm tough."

Hoyt carried her through the darkened house. Enough light came in from the big security lights outside to keep the rooms from utter darkness, and Hoyt had lived here his whole life, so he could probably walk through it with his eyes closed.

"I like when you fuss like that, Miss Eadie. Makes me think you like me just a little."

She heard the smile in his voice, and it took everything she had to keep back the words *I love you* that were trying to crowd out.

"I thought you wanted me to fuss," she

said instead, then immediately felt like a coward. ‘‘And of course I like you.’’

As cowardly as it felt to avoid the words, the last thing she wanted was to say the words, ‘‘I love you,’’ then have Hoyt casually repeat them back to her only because he thought he should. Or because he thought she expected him to.

Eadie was glad the house was dark or he might have seen what she felt for him on her face. She’d always managed to hide her feelings from him, but things had changed drastically between them. They were at ease with each other in so many ways that her guard had dropped. But although she felt a significant amount of security after the ceremony today, she also knew the safest thing to do, for Hoyt as well as for her, was to wait until he said the words first.

Hoyt carried her all the way into the master bedroom then lowered her to her feet beside the bed before he moved away to switch on a lamp. When he turned back, his dark eyes gleamed in the soft light. His gaze made a slow sweep of her and grew solemn.

‘‘Did I tell you how beautiful you are in that dress?’’

Eadie felt her face flush. ‘‘Did I tell you how handsome you are in that tuxedo? And I noticed you kept the coat on most of the time. I meant to let you know you didn’t have to, but I…liked the way you looked. You look good in black.’’

Hoyt grinned. ‘‘We both just found a few nerves, didn’t we?’’

‘‘Yes.’’

‘‘Then let’s go back to what we know,’’ he said. Now some of his frequent crankiness resurfaced, but she could tell it was faked. ‘‘Help me out here, would you?’’

It was something he’d said to her several times before, and brought back what he’d said the night he’d proposed: *We get along…in our way.*

Eadie smiled a little but a tide of shyness swept through her as she walked to him and complied. The coat came off smoothly, but Hoyt gently took it and gave it a cavalier toss to an armchair. His dark eyes glittered down at her.

‘‘How ’bout this collar next? And you can just toss that cravatty thing in the garbage tomorrow for all I care.’’

Eadie reached up to unsnap the ‘‘cravatty’’ tie that was folded under the tux shirt collar. She gave it a toss in the general direction of the jacket before she started to work on buttons of the shirt.

The backs of her fingers were pleasantly scorched from contact with Hoyt's hot shirtfront, and she was pleased to note again that the hair on his tanned chest was neither too little nor too much. She'd tried not to stare at the doctor's office the other day, but the sight of Hoyt without his shirt had been burned on her memory.

When she got down to the cummerbund, she made a gentle search for the fasteners and removed it.

"My turn to catch up," Hoyt said, and his voice was almost a rasp. As if the little bit of undressing had already affected him. Eadie glanced up briefly to see the faint fire in his dark eyes then looked away to turn so he could open the buttons at the back of her dress.

There weren't quite two dozen of them, more like twenty. *Exactly* twenty. Eadie's brain kept count because with every one he unbuttoned, the sensual tingles that flared began to flutter through her like quivery streamers. When he finished, Hoyt placed his big warm palms against her bare skin and skimmed the gown off her shoulders.

Eadie automatically caught the bodice before it fell below her breasts, but Hoyt's hands came around and closed over the backs of hers. He eased against her and her lashes drifted closed in pure anticipation when she felt his warm breath against her neck. And then his lips began to first tenderly nibble and then press slow, lingering kisses on the soft flesh there.

He gradually lowered her hands and the bodice fell to her waist before he moved back enough for the fabric to whisper to the floor at her feet. Eadie thought he'd kiss her again, but instead his arms tightened around her.

"I've rushed you, Eadie, and I'm a lucky cuss, 'cause you let me." He pressed a kiss against her ear that almost made her knees buckle.

When he finished, his warm breath gusted gently across her cheek. "But I've got you now, so maybe I can slow down a little. As much as I'd like to make love to you tonight, I want you to decide when. I can't promise not to try to seduce you, but if you'd be more at ease just sharing this bed tonight, then we'd have to stop now while I've still got a few good intentions left.''

Trust Hoyt to be blunt, but what got to her was his sensitivity. The stark contrast between this loud, domineering man and his strong streak of sensitivity made her suddenly emotional. It took her a moment to get control of her voice.

''I appreciate the chance for things to happen a little more naturally,'' she got out.

Hoyt's arms tightened. ''Then will you share my bed tonight, Eadie?''

''Yes.''

Hoyt kissed her cheek before he pressed his against it. ''Then to show you what a great husband I am, I'll let you use the shower in here. I'll use one of the others tonight, since it's so late. Then I'll be interested to see what you picked out to wear, though I hope it's not too thin or too... skimpy.''

Eadie smiled at the mock desperation in his tone at that last. ''I think I can guarantee that.''

Hoyt straightened, then turned her in his arms before his dark head lowered and he caught her lips in a hot kiss that made her head spin. All too soon he brought it to an end, and his voice was again a rasp.

"I reckon that's enough for now." He loosened his arms and stepped back. As he did, his fingers trailed under her arms then caught her fingers. His dark gaze went down the length of her slip to where it stopped just above her white pumps.

Eadie felt heat trail along that path, but the slip revealed no more than outlines, so she was remarkably unself-conscious. So far.

"Be sure you put that slip in a drawer you'll never open," he ordered gruffly, and that was no pretense. "I think I've seen your legs about four times in my life."

Then he released her fingers and turned away to cross the carpet to the hall.

Eadie had gotten the bit of time she'd hoped for after all, and she couldn't help wondering how far it was between the affection Hoyt genuinely seemed to have for her and the love she so craved.

On the other hand, Hoyt was very experienced at romancing women, so he was good at this. Maybe too good. And he'd never stayed in a relationship for any significant length of time, so instead of this being special and unique with her, it might very well be Hoyt's usual...method.

Eadie's heart sank a little. She picked up her dress and took a moment to inspect the place the little girl had taken hold of. Miss Ed had done a fast repair on an unraveling thread, and from the looks of it, the fix had held. Hoyt had gotten two other little girls to go on a search for the two pearls Miss Ed estimated had come off, and they'd found them on the sheet beneath Eadie's chair on the hearth.

Eadie carried the long dress into the big walk-in closet to hang it up, then did the same with Hoyt's coat. When she came out, she collected her things from the dresser where she'd put them yesterday before she paused. Ever a sentimentalist, she retrieved the despised "cravatty thing" from the chair and tucked it away in a corner of her lingerie drawer before she hurried into the big bathroom.

Since she was leery of Hoyt returning to their bedroom before she was ready for bed, Eadie finished in record time. The shyness she felt would be worse if she walked out in her nightclothes to an audience, but it probably wouldn't faze Hoyt since he must have done it before. Because he was never shy or self-conscious about anything, it was better for her to be the audience, at least for a time or two.

After what Hoyt had said about her long slip, she hoped he wouldn't be too disappointed that the white satin gown and robe she'd bought was full-length. On the other hand, his request about what she wore to bed would be easily fulfilled, though she suspected he'd show at least a hint of macho dismay when he saw how well.

Just then, Eadie heard a door open somewhere down the hall and panicked a little, fidgeting with the robe's tie belt as she considered whether or not to take it off and slip into bed before Hoyt got there. It didn't seem right to do that yet though.

Just a bit more than a week ago, she'd worked part-time for Hoyt and she'd never even seen the private areas of his house before he'd gotten hurt. Now she was married to him. Eadie again felt the soft jolt of the suddenness of all this and wondered if she'd ever get past that.

But then he walked into the room and she felt her face go hot. He was wearing dark blue pajama bottoms and her gaze flashed up from those to note that the cut on his side was healing well before her gaze lifted to his face. He came to a halt two feet away and she felt an earthquake of excitement.

The sheer masculinity of the man had never seemed more blatant or more starkly threatening. Or appealing. His expression was stony, but his dark eyes were alive with an intensity that might have knocked her back a step if she'd been standing just an inch or so closer.

"Ah, Eadie," he breathed as that intense gaze went down the front of her, lingering and tracing here and there, and somehow making her feel it like a touch. His voice lowered. "By damn, woman."

For a moment Eadie couldn't tell if he was about to comment on the fact that he still couldn't see her legs, but there was nothing at all critical in the frank appraisal he'd given her. Was *still* giving her as that dark gaze floated slowly upward.

"I picked the best." He gave his head a shake, as if he was a little in wonder, and Eadie felt a pang of doubt because she couldn't truly believe she looked quite that good to a man who'd dated so many beauties.

"Oh, Hoyt," she scolded softly, but then he reached to take her hands.

"Oh, Hoyt what?"

Eadie's gaze self-consciously fled his, and she tried to defy the warm, callused grip that made her feel so weak. "You don't have to make adoring comments."

"Don't I always tell you the truth?"

"This isn't our normal area of conversation."

"You think I'm lying?"

"I think you're being sweet, yes."

Hoyt tightened his grip to prompt her to look up at him. He looked so sexy. Drop dead sexy. His voice was a growl.

"Then let's get it straight up front. I don't lie, Eadie. Not even in the bedroom." Now he grinned. "So, do you think I look as good in dark blue as I did in black today?"

Hoyt's grin widened and she giggled. "Do you want me to tell you how...how h-handsome I think you are?" His grin, his nearness, and the wonderful pleasure that just holding his hands gave her, was affecting her more by the second.

His grin faded and he looked a little insulted. ''It's not like I'm fishin' for compliments.''

His look said he *was* and Eadie giggled again. ''You're very handsome. You always are.''

''Hah. You can't say it with a straight face, can you?''

Hoyt was not only straight-faced now, he looked cranky again, but she could tell it was faked. ''Not when you make me giggle.''

''Here I thought you'd be a serious woman, especially at a time like this when my vanity needs to be propped up. You don't think a groom wants his bride to flatter him a little?''

Eadie giggled yet again, then made the effort to be serious. ''Oh, Hoyt, you know you're handsome. You've probably already guessed that I think you're very handsome, and that I've always thought so.''

Hoyt gave her a narrow glare that was just a touch annoyed. And it seemed genuine this time. ''And just how could I be expected to guess that? You've spent more time looking at Mike and Mose than you ever have at me.''

"I have a good memory for faces," she teased and Hoyt's cranky expression eased into a smile. He liked to be teased, but gently. "Gawking at you all afternoon hasn't been part of how it's been between us in the past."

"None of this has, but I like the change already, Eadie. How 'bout you?"

Eadie sobered as he moved close. "Me, too."

Hoyt's smile eased and his voice lowered. "Then why don't we do one or two more new things, like get that robe off, turn down the covers, and slip into bed together."

It wasn't really a question, but Eadie gave a small nod of agreement. "All right."

"May I?"

Eadie's gaze wavered from the growing fire in his and she gave another nod. Hoyt released one of her hands to reach for the belt of her robe. But he did little more than hook a finger in it and give a tug before he bent down and caught her lips in a brief, light kiss.

Then Hoyt released her other hand and Eadie felt the robe slip to her elbows before he dragged the satin sleeves the rest of the way off and ended the kiss. He lifted his head and tossed the robe across the foot of the bed. They were no longer touching.

"How's this so far?" he asked.

"It's fine."

"I'd say so, too. Which side of the bed for you?" His tone was conversational now, which put her a little more at ease.

"Which side for you?" she asked back.

"I like this side, but I'm not choosy."

"Good. I like the other."

"Simple then." Hoyt leaned away and grabbed the bedspread to flip it down. "After you."

CHAPTER EIGHT

AFTER you…

Eadie couldn't miss the glitter of amusement and male anticipation in Hoyt's dark, dark eyes, and felt her heart quiver with a wild combination of maidenly fear and feminine excitement. As long as she'd been in love with Hoyt, she'd never truly thought clearly about sexual intimacy. Whatever he'd just said about waiting, did he truly mean to wait?

I can't promise not to try to seduce you…

Despite what he'd said about being willing to wait, he'd also said that. She was about to get into bed with one of the sexiest men in Texas. The reminder was just the sort of thing that made Eadie realize how far out of her depth she really was.

Until that moment, she'd handled Hoyt's blustery moods with a kind of aplomb that was always calmly forbearing, sometimes indulgent, most often diplomatic, but always, always she'd done those things with an attitude of weary female superiority that forgave him for being male and at the mercy of his domineering and sometimes thickheaded biology.

It shocked her to realize she'd had that kind of female arrogance. It shocked her even more to find that she suddenly couldn't seem to find a scrap of it to ward him off and somehow make him seem more…manageable. She seemed to have lost her courage, too.

Eadie abruptly turned away and walked around the foot of the bed to the far side. Though she knew Hoyt had expected her to get in on his side of the bed then move across the mattress, that was a recipe for even more self-consciousness. It was one thing to face him wearing only a thin sheath of satin. It was another to turn her back on him and crawl across the mattress, particularly since the elegant nightgown dipped far lower in the back than in front.

She got into bed without looking over at him. Hoyt must have watched every move she'd made—she'd *felt* his gaze on her—because he didn't get in on his side until she'd pulled the comforter up. The weight of his big body settling beside her and the radiant heat of his nearness warmed her from shoulder to toe, particularly when he pulled his half of the covers to his chest.

Eadie had never shared a bed before, aside from childhood sleepovers. And Hoyt was no middle school girlfriend. She'd wanted to be with him though, wanted it for years. She'd not had a prayer of ever having so much as a casual date with him until a few short days ago. Now she was married to him.

Hoyt belonged to her now, belonged *with* her. It was at least something that no other woman before her could claim, though that difference was hers only because of a ceremony and a piece of paper. And yet that ceremony and piece of paper were far more valuable and binding than any other private commitment a man and a woman could make in life. The only thing more valuable and binding was to bring children into the shelter and protection of that legal commitment.

Hoyt shifted beside her and the bedside lamp went off. Eadie might have relaxed then because he could no longer see her face, but the darkness made her even more sharply aware that his arm was little more than a minimal two inches from hers.

"You're stiff as a board, Eadie," he growled. "You scared of me now?"

"No."

"But you're wondering if I'm gonna suddenly turn into an octopus, huh?"

Eadie smiled at the image. "I trust you."

"I said you could," he said tersely.

She felt him shift again and his hand found hers to grip it warmly.

"I like to think we've been friends," he said then. "Maybe that's just me takin' it wrong, but if we really aren't friends yet, I'm saying I want us to be." He paused. "How's that?"

Deep affection welled up and it was all Eadie could do not to put her free hand over the back of his. The small war she fought was because she didn't want to distract either of them from what he might say next. And he did have more to say, she could sense it.

Instead she said quietly, "I want that, too."

"All right then. I've got three things to say that I might tell a close friend."

Eadie smiled. Though she'd sensed this, she should have known Hoyt would preface their talk like that. In many ways, she appreciated that he was anything but the silent type, even when a lot of the things he said put her on the spot. It was certainly true that he'd confided a lot of things to her over the years, and that a lot of those things had made her love him even more.

"Yes?"

Hoyt didn't keep her waiting, so she knew he must have been thinking about this for a while.

"First off, you and Miss Ed are the only females who've ever been in this room. So if you're thinkin' this bed has been used for anything but sleep, you'd be wrong."

Because she caught the sincerity in what he'd said, Eadie managed not to giggle at the way he'd put it. And it was good to know that she was the first woman he'd brought here.

"Thanks for telling me."

Though he'd mentioned having three things to say, it was several moments before he went on to the next one. And when he did go on, Eadie couldn't miss his defensive tone.

"Second. Whatever you think about how I've acted with the women I've gone out with, I've not slept with one in a long time. Not that I've ever actually *slept* with any woman, but I figure you'll get what I mean without spelling it out. Someday I'll tell you when it was that I wised up, but not now."

Eadie laid in the dark taking that in, amused again at how he'd put it, but touched that he'd wanted her to know. She hoped it was true.

"I appreciate that you told me," she said at last.

Hoyt released the breath he must have been holding, but his voice was grim. "So you're too polite to call me a liar. I wouldn't blame you if you did. I know my own reputation."

"I accepted the fact that you're experienced a long time ago, Hoyt," she said quietly. "I expect you to be faithful to me from here on."

"I swore that today, too," he said gruffly. "You know I keep my word."

"I know, Hoyt."

"Like I said the other night, you know a lot of things about me that I didn't guess.

All those times I thought you weren't paying attention, you were.'' His chuckle was warm. ''You were just cool about it, not letting on. That can drive a man crazy, you know.''

Eadie didn't remark on that. It not only pleased her to hear that she'd been able to keep so much to herself and therefore hadn't revealed her true feelings for Hoyt, but she was especially pleased to hear that he'd been bothered by her apparent indifference, though that probably didn't mean what she wished it did.

Hoyt was a man who naturally attracted attention everywhere he went, so it must be unusual for him to come across someone who seemed a bit oblivious. In that she and Miss Ed had provided a healthy balance for an ego that might take too much for granted otherwise.

Eadie wasn't sure if that idea was more evidence of her just realized female arrogance, but she sensed it was time to move away from the subject of just how *much* she'd noticed about him all along...before she was lured into confessing what she'd felt about it.

"You said you had three things you might say to a close friend."

"That was only two, huh?" He paused another moment then went on. "Number three's a question. I'm a light sleeper, so I was wondering…you don't snore, do you?"

The question surprised a little laugh out of her. "What a rude question on a wedding night!" She reached over to playfully pinch his thick wrist, but it was so hard with muscle that there wasn't much to pinch. "Do *you?*"

Hoyt chuckled, and it was a wonderful masculine sound that wrapped snugly around her.

"Just trying to lighten things up, but maybe doin' a bad job of it. You hardly make enough noise for me to know you're in the room most of the time, so I wouldn't mind if you did snore. In fact, I can't think of a thing about you that wouldn't be all right with me, Eadie."

It was a sweet thing to say, and it thrilled her, but her instinct was to keep that to herself. "What if I'm balky?"

"You know I like to bellyache about

that, but I don't mind much. I've always liked you, Eadie.''

Her soft, ''I've always liked you, too,'' just slipped out and Eadie bit her lip, appalled at how easy it had been. But then Hoyt spoke and she realized he'd not assigned much significance to her admission.

''Then why don't you lean over here and kiss me good-night? We don't want to start anything too big tonight, so it can't be much.'' He paused. ''And just so you'll know, it's fine with me if you want to take the lead in things like that. I'm not picky about who starts it, just so one of us does.''

Eadie hesitated a moment before she complied, amused by the way Hoyt often worded things. She thought of them as blunt euphemisms. Just one more thing she loved about him. Eadie pulled her hand from his and turned toward him to rise up on her elbow.

Her next hesitation was because she was reluctant to put her hand on his bare chest. Doing that suddenly seemed more intimate in the dark. Eadie compromised by putting her fingers on his lean cheek as she leaned over and cautiously touched her lips to his.

Though she wasn't quite a novice at

kissing after the past week, this kiss was the very first she'd initiated. The emotion involved in the act of making that tender contact and the craving to do it well enough to please him, made her a little bolder than she'd intended but she couldn't seem to help it.

She made the kiss go on a little longer because Hoyt's firm, warm mouth felt so nice that it was a sharp disappointment when she realized it was time to end this. She didn't mean to give him the idea that she was ready for more, though by the time she drew away, her hope for the first time between them to happen after a love confession was beginning to waver.

"That was sweet, Eadie," he breathed after she drew back. "Like you."

He hadn't moved a muscle while she'd kissed him, but now that she'd pulled back a little, his arm slipped behind her and he settled her against his side. The thin layer of satin between them was almost like being skin to skin. Almost. And now there was no place for her hand to go but on his chest.

Hoyt released a gusty breath of satisfaction. ‘‘Feels good to have you there, darlin’. Good night.’’

‘‘Good night.’’

It was all Eadie could do to keep the hand on his chest still and to keep from rubbing her cheek against the hard warm flesh of his shoulder. She couldn’t see the digital readout of the alarm clock on the bedside table so she didn’t know how long they both laid there together in the dark. Though neither of them said another word and hardly made a move, they were both wide-awake.

Eadie was aware of every beat of his heart and hers, and every self-conscious breath they each took. However long they’d known each other and worked together, and despite the fact that they were married and were now sharing a bed, there was a formidable wall of restraint between them.

She suddenly sensed there was more to that wall of restraint than her reluctance to have sex without love, or Hoyt’s determination not to pressure a woman who’d once been roughed up on a bad date.

That was the moment it struck her that the kind of closeness and ease they needed now was the very thing that a proper and long courtship was meant to achieve. The fact that they hadn't had a proper courtship made their hasty choice seem even more risky than ever.

And yet Eadie didn't quite regret that they'd rushed things. She'd been in the right place at the right time with the man she'd loved for years, and she'd selfishly not been able to turn this down.

Heaven help her, she'd wanted this, wanted him. And the chance of a lifetime had dropped in her lap. She could no more have refused to take it than she could have refused her next breath. For better or worse, there had to be a way to make this marriage a good one, however it had started.

Hoyt did genuinely like her, she didn't doubt that, and it thrilled her to hear him indicate that he'd liked her far more than she'd ever suspected. And he'd chosen her over his beauties. That had to mean something, and she meant to make the most of it.

After what must have been a good hour or more, the day finally caught up with her, and she slipped off to sleep.

* * *

Eadie awoke early that next morning. She was wrapped around the most wonderful heat and for a few moments she drifted, too uncommonly comfortable and secure to want to move away from the source.

Moments later, she realized she was lying half over Hoyt's big, hard body. Her head was on his chest, her arm rested on his waist, and her right thigh lay heavily across both of his. His words from the night before came back to her.

I'm a light sleeper...

Eadie could hear the slow beat of Hoyt's heart and guessed he was still asleep. His big body was slack, particularly compared to the tension in him last night as they'd waited for sleep. The house was still except for the faint sound of the central air-conditioning when it cycled on to blow cool air through the vents, so almost any move she made would disturb the silence.

In truth, it wasn't quite feminine shyness that made her eager to move away without waking him. Despite Hoyt's generous compliments yesterday and last night, Eadie's instinct was to look her best at all times now, particularly first thing in the morning, so that was vanity rather than shyness. And he'd seemed unhappy about her disheveled appearance the other night, so that was still fresh in her mind.

The fact was, Hoyt was used to being with women who were so spectacular looking that they'd be gorgeous anytime, even first thing in the morning. Eadie wasn't about to let Hoyt get a close look at her first moments of the day, at least not this soon. Perhaps it wouldn't be quite such a risk once the beauties began to fade from his memory, but she wouldn't count on that.

Eadie was just about to move when Hoyt shifted and his hand settled on the thigh that lay across his.

"G'mornin'."

Eadie's soft, "Good morning," was more squeak than speech. Not only was her thigh over his, but the hem of her nightgown was bunched hip high beneath the covers. She slipped her hand off his chest to pull it down a little.

She'd no more than done that when Hoyt turned, gently pressing her to her back to loom over her. His dark eyes gleamed down into hers and her own felt like saucers.

Hoyt's dark hair was sleep tousled, and his jaw was shaded with beard stubble. She'd never seen him unshaven or mussy, but the almost savage look about him was a picture of raw masculinity, and she felt wonderfully soft and weak and female. As his gaze studied her face, she felt a hot flush go over her from scalp to toes. Hoyt's voice was still rough from sleep.

"I coulda been wakin' up to you a long time ago, Eadie Donovan. I was a fool to wait."

And then his head descended and his lips settled firmly on hers. Eadie didn't have time to feel self-conscious about the kiss or to dwell on what he'd said about being a fool.

Hoyt's warm mouth was masterful, and from the first touch, nothing else registered but the feel of his lips on hers and the staggering response of her body. When he suddenly drew away, Eadie felt deprived, and she opened dazed eyes to his fiery gaze.

"That's about all I can handle right now and still make it out of bed before noon," he said then gave a wry grin. "Unless..."

There was no way to miss the hopeful

lift in that one word, or the deep quiver it set off inside her.

''Guess not,'' he supplied good-naturedly before she could answer. ''I reckon you'd be shy in the daylight.''

Eadie couldn't prevent a small smile at Hoyt's lighthearted—and on target—assessment.

''Might as well get up and find some clothes,'' he went on. ''Miss Ed's probably got coffee going.'' With that, he turned away and got out of bed. Eadie did the same, then reached for her robe.

''What plans do you have for today?'' she asked, then glanced his way. Though his bare-chested masculinity was still a bit overwhelming, Eadie couldn't help feasting her eyes on him while he wasn't looking directly at her.

''Having you to myself,'' he said as he flipped up the bedspread to cover the pillows, as if he regularly did that before Miss Ed could see to making the bed properly. ''Anything special you'd like to do?'' he asked before he glanced her way.

His dark eyes noted the robe she held but hadn't put on before his gaze rose to take in the sight of her without it. His sensual appraisal and her shyness about it prompted her to again wish for the kind of closeness and ease with Hoyt that had seemed so absent last night as they'd waited for sleep. The kind of closeness and ease that felt even more absent under his male scrutiny.

Real life wasn't much like the usual date or formal outing, so it seemed to her that doing a few low-key everyday things might bring them closer more quickly. Besides, Hoyt had dated for years, often taking one girlfriend or another on a romantic date or to a formal event, but she hadn't heard that any of his women had ever just hung around with him at the ranch.

Eadie smiled a little, determined to set herself apart from the others. "Do we have to do something special? I've never seen much of Donovan Ranch away from the house."

Hoyt's wandering gaze shifted to hers and narrowed a moment before he gave her a chiding look that was an obvious sham.

"You just eat, sleep and breathe ranching, don't you?"

"'Fraid so. Think you can adjust?"

"Oh, yeah. Today I'll show you Donovan, tomorrow we'll go to Webb. But then I want to take you dancing in San Antonio, stay overnight so you can get in some serious shopping if you want. I've heard about wives who drag their husbands through malls, wearing out boot leather and running up credit card bills. It's time I got some stories of my own to brag about."

Eadie felt a niggle of unease. She'd thought when she'd asked that they not go on a honeymoon right away, that Hoyt understood she couldn't take much time off until fall. She'd been so swept away by Hoyt and busy before the wedding that she hadn't gone into detail about just how little time she could afford to spend away from Webb Ranch these next weeks.

But it was obvious Hoyt hadn't realized she'd meant to go back to work at her place in the next day or so, or he wouldn't be making plans to go to San Antonio. She had a couple of friends covering for her today and tomorrow morning with chores, but she didn't have enough time or energy to swap chores too many times.

Plus, she and Hoyt hadn't discussed her part-time work for him, but she could hardly take wages from him now that she was his wife. The loss of that bit of income made it even more important to avoid hired help.

"We probably do need to talk about work this week," she said, trying to sound casual about it, but wanting to hint at what was coming as she turned to walk to the dresser for underthings.

"Work?"

Eadie heard the flat tone in the word but stayed calm as she gathered clothes. She turned to give Hoyt a conciliatory smile.

"Do you mind if we talk about it later? In the meantime, do you want to use the bathroom first or can I?"

Hoyt made a vague gesture. "I'll use the one next door."

Eadie made her escape, grateful to find a little privacy to organize herself and think of a way to handle the subject of work.

CHAPTER NINE

OF COURSE Hoyt was used to taking time away from Donovan Ranch if he chose to. He certainly had enough people working for him to make that possible, and he never had to worry about money. It wasn't as though he didn't realize her ranch was small and her resources limited, but Eadie could easily imagine him lending her cowhands who were on his payroll and then not allowing her to reimburse him for their wages.

Not that she could afford to pay full-time wages, but she couldn't let Hoyt pay them for her, especially when she was still uncertain about whether to sell out or hang on and keep trying to get her place back into the black.

She'd never wanted Hoyt to know too much about her small operation while things had been rough but now that they were married, he'd know enough about how she spent her days to figure it out. She'd focused so much on getting through the wedding that she hadn't let herself think too much about the subject.

She'd been caught up in marrying Hoyt before he changed his mind. As foolish as that had been, she'd not been able to be sensible. Ideally she should have risked it and put off the wedding until she'd made a decision about her place. Because she hadn't had the patience to wait, she'd have to deal with whatever complications it might cause between them now.

The best thing to do at this point was to lay it out and mark some clear boundaries. The last thing she wanted was for Hoyt to think she'd married him for his money. He'd been up-front about his reasons for marrying her, and though she couldn't be up-front about her real reason for marrying him, she didn't want him to think, even for a moment, that she'd married him to save her ranch.

And there was also her worry that things might not work out between them. Though Hoyt was a man of his word, she couldn't help but think about the number of women he'd had in his life. He'd never stayed interested for more than a couple months. And though he apparently hadn't loved any of them, he wasn't in love with her either.

They had a pleasant breakfast in the dining room, and they read through the paper and talked about a variety of things. If she hadn't known better, Eadie might have figured that Hoyt had forgotten about her mention of work. But she'd been around him long enough to sense a faint impatience about him, as if he was reluctant to mention something that might cause a disagreement on their first morning of married life. She also sensed he was determined to settle the issue.

And settle it *his* way, of course, and that accounted for the tension in his faint impatience. Eadie saw that as a sign that her lay-down-the-law husband might be a bit leery of how she'd take being dictated to now that they were married.

"I wonder if Leah's had the baby yet?" Eadie remarked later as they walked into the den with their coffee.

Eadie chose one of the wing chairs in front of Hoyt's desk, and sat back with her coffee while he walked to a cabinet at the side of the big room. They'd allegedly come in here to get Eadie a map of Donovan Ranch for quick reference while they went on a driving tour, but she knew the main reason was to discuss work.

"I'll give Reece a call later," Hoyt said, then brought out a map and carried it over to her. He angled the other wing chair so they were facing each other before he sat down. Eadie set her coffee aside and opened the map for a look.

Hoyt pointed out a few things to help orient her, but they'd go over it in more detail once they were on the range, at least the part nearest the headquarters. When he finished, she refolded the map before she reached for her coffee. Hoyt gave her another moment before he zeroed in.

"What was that you said about work?" He was trying to be mild, but she couldn't miss the hint of disapproval in his tone.

"We haven't had a lot of time this past week to discuss the day-to-day things, have we?" she asked, trying to ease into the subject. She still wasn't sure of the best way to handle this but since Hoyt seemed to have already guessed what was coming, she might as well get right to the point.

"I can't take much time away from

Webb Ranch right now,'' she began, ''which was the reason for delaying a honeymoon. I might be able to go to San Antonio in the next couple of weeks, but this week I need to make up for some of the past three days, along with keeping up with the regular work. As soon as I get ahead, we might go.''

Hoyt's dark gaze searched hers. ''You make it sound like you don't plan to be around here much.''

''Of course I will.''

''When?''

''Early morning, supper and at night.'' Eadie tried not to cringe at how that sounded, especially because of the somber look Hoyt was giving her. At least it was somber and not angry. Not yet. ''My place will take the same amount of my time it always has, just as Donovan Ranch will yours.''

''Every day?''

''That depends on whether I'll still be working for you three afternoons a week, though I expect that to end since I'm no longer an employee.''

''Huh.''

Eadie had been around Hoyt long

enough to know that "huh" usually meant he disapproved of something but wasn't ready to specifically say so yet. He sometimes did that when he expected the other person to realize he disapproved and of course, along with that realization, change their way of thinking to line up with his before he had to actually insist. Since he most often expressed his opinions bluntly, this was his occasional effort to seem reasonable.

The issue of boss/employee—and especially the one about where she spent her time—were potential disagreements. Perhaps big ones. Hoyt was still old-fashioned in most ways, but what groom wanted his first day of married life to be a series of disagreements?

"What about when the babies start coming?"

Eadie shrugged and set her cup on the front edge of the desk. "I hope to make a decision about my place before too much longer."

"Will you hire some full-time folks to handle the work?"

"That depends on how things go the next few months. Since I'm married now and we plan to have children, it'll have to do well enough to cover its own expenses, including wages and benefits for hired help.''

Hoyt's gaze pushed into hers. ''Which is why you swap chores with a couple other small outfits now instead of hiring help.''

''That's right.''

Hoyt reached over to give her knee a pat in a manner that fairly shouted that the issue was settled. ''You'll run yourself ragged doing that now. And there's no reason,'' he said briskly. ''I'll send over a couple of my men to take care of the worst of things this week, and work out a permanent schedule later.''

He started to rise as if he'd solved the problem and meant to rush them on to their tour before she could protest. Eadie tried not to show her dismay, but instead leaned back in her chair in a way that told him she wasn't as eager to rush past this issue as he was.

''That's very generous, Hoyt, but you know it's unwise to use money and resources from one operation to prop up another. If my ranch can't pay its own way, I'll sell out.''

Her soft declaration made him scowl as he sat back down.

"I thought this marriage was a partnership?" Hoyt abruptly stopped then, as if he realized how gruff that sounded. He made a visible effort to relax and went on a little more mildly. "And you'll want to pass on your daddy's place to our kids. If we have enough of 'em, we'll need to have plenty to pass on."

Oh, he was trying so hard to get his way and appear mellow, though Eadie knew he was anything but. Especially on the issue of heritage. It was clear he was just as intent on passing on her heritage as he was his own, and she loved him for it. Nevertheless, Webb Ranch was in trouble, so it wasn't quite the same as Donovan Ranch, which had been in Hoyt's family for generations.

"I didn't marry you to have you bail me out of my money troubles," she said.

Hoyt's brows curved into cranky whorls, and the look on his face told her she'd offended him. "I married you to have you bail me out of my troubles and give me a family."

"I married you for the same family, so we're even."

Now Hoyt's aggravation began to show a little more. "You don't think a husband and wife oughta share everything they've got with each other, including money and resources? Don't they help each other out? Fix things and give things?"

He paused a moment then his gaze sharpened meaningfully to emphasize his point. "*Accept* help or money with some kind of *grace* when the other one wants to be good to them?"

As she'd expected, Hoyt was upset, though he kept most of it contained.

"I know you mean well, Hoyt, and you're one of the most generous people I know—"

"But you won't let me help out," he cut in. "Would you at least let me have a look so I've got a better idea of what you're dealing with?"

Eadie felt her face flush. "The truth is, I'm a little embarrassed to be in this fix. It might even be past the point of no return. I'd like to come out of it with something if I decide to sell."

Hoyt's dark gaze searched hers and then

gentled, and his stern expression mellowed, as if he knew what it cost her to admit that.

"Hell, Eadie, it's tough to turn a profit on a small place, especially if you're working it alone. Plus I figure inheritance taxes set you back after your momma passed on, and maybe water troubles, since you mentioned not using the dishwasher the other day. You've got plenty of graze to turn a profit, but maybe not enough water to carry more cattle, is that right?"

Eadie felt her heart squeeze a little at his automatic rejection of the idea that she was at fault for not doing better, but she was compelled to take responsibility.

"It could also be that I'm not very good at ranching."

"Hell with that. Taxes make it hard to pass down to family, and we've had near drought conditions for too long, not to mention the rising cost of staying in business. Troubles come along every day—your tractor for one—but you're carrying the whole job on a place that isn't diverse enough yet to take too many troubles at once. Then there's the market."

He was making good points, but Eadie

knew others who'd coped much better with most of the same troubles she'd faced.

"That's why Donovan Ranch is invested in more than just land and cattle," he went on, "and has been since my great-granddaddy's day. Oil provided a hefty share of Donovan prosperity. And you've been workin' alone. That limits you right there, but now you won't have those limits."

Eadie felt such a rush of emotion that she had to look away. "Oh, Hoyt..."

He leaned forward to take her hand. "When I got cut up, you said you'd do just about anything for me," he pointed out. "What if it was me who was in your fix? Going by what you said, you'd do anything to help me, wouldn't you? Well, it's the same for me. Giving you a hand wouldn't put a noticeable dent in my wallet, even if I bought you a new tractor, paid off your bank notes and drilled a couple new wells."

Eadie felt the warm strength in his hand undermine her control even more. She had a hard time answering in a voice that didn't sound choked. Her eyes were stinging with love and she wasn't sure how much of it she wanted Hoyt to see.

"Being able to do those things doesn't necessarily mean it's wise to do them, or fair to you." She made herself look at him. "I can't let you do it."

"Then we'll keep a tally," he persisted. "When Webb Ranch is operating at a profit, you can pay back the cost. You won't need personal income from Webb anyway now that you've got a rich husband."

Eadie shook her head again. "I can't let you do it. I'll just...put it on the market and be done with it."

Hoyt's fingers tightened gently. "Pride looks mighty foolish when you put it up against common sense, Eadie. I could invest and become your partner."

"Hoyt," she said quietly, "wouldn't you have just as much trouble swallowing your pride as I do mine?" She smiled to soften that, though he didn't seem to have taken offense. But he didn't back off either.

"Webb Ranch needs to stay in the family," he insisted. "If you're gonna be stubborn about it, then let me buy it outright. Then you won't have the hardship of trying to handle it alone while we're trying to start our family. If I do buy it, I'd keep it intact as Webb Ranch and have you to oversee it. That way, you'd have time to learn more about Donovan interests so you could handle the whole shebang if something happened to me.''

Eadie couldn't maintain contact with his dark gaze. She couldn't bring herself to turn him down flat, but she didn't want to accept his offer. At least not yet. A couple days away from her place made her eager to get back to it and take up the struggle to keep it. Perhaps she'd feel differently later, when she was tired and frustrated, and feeling discouraged. Or once she got pregnant.

Hoyt was right, they would be starting their family soon, though she hoped to wait until she felt surer of things between them. But she already knew there was no way she could keep up the hard schedule and demanding physical work she'd been living with, especially in the past few months, if she was pregnant.

''Would you give me some time to think about it?''

Hoyt didn't answer until she looked at him. Oh, how handsome he was, and how dear. The tenderness in his eyes made her feel almost…loved.

"All right." His low words weren't quite the relief they first seemed to be when he added, "I hope the reason you want to hold off on a decision isn't because you're waiting to see if things work out between us or not."

It shocked her a little to hear him say that. Not only had he pegged her secret worry, but he gave the impression that *he* might be worried she was doing just that. But then common sense kicked in and she realized he might have had a wisp or two of doubt about their marriage himself, so that didn't mean he was worried about it in the same way she was.

After the big production yesterday, it would be quite an embarrassment—and a blow to Hoyt's pride about being a man of his word—if he had to divorce her and find another wife. A task that would be even more embarrassing and damaging to his pride if she was the one who ended this and moved home to Webb Ranch. Was this proof that being dumped by Celeste had left a mark?

Though Eadie hadn't detected even an

inkling of doubt in him about their marriage, this was Hoyt Donovan, and until a little more than a week ago, he'd been the man no one expected to ever marry and settle down. And they'd married in a huge rush. Hadn't she been anxious to marry him quickly because she'd been afraid he might change his mind if she didn't jump at the chance?

"What you've offered is…sudden, Hoyt, and generous, but it's a lot to think about. And to tell you the truth, the changes between us are already a little overwhelming. Could you give me time at Webb this week while I think it all over in light of your proposals?"

"How 'bout we pack some clothes and spend the nights at your house this week? I could give you a hand, we could have Miss Ed bring our meals, but we'd be there by ourselves." One corner of his handsome mouth curved up. "You'd be the boss, and I'd be your hardworking cowhand."

The thought, *Be careful what you wish for,* made a quick pass through her mind. She'd thought doing everyday things together might give them the closeness they lacked before full intimacy, and there was nothing more everyday than working with Hoyt at her place, day in and day out. It wouldn't be at all like her coming here three afternoons a week to work for him, because he'd only been around about half the time while she'd been working. At her place, they'd be alone together twenty-four hours a day.

Though she could think of dozens of ways her small operation compared unfavorably to the mammoth, well-managed one Hoyt ran, and her house was just a simple one instead of the showplace he owned, Hoyt was no snob. The problem would be preventing him from spending money on anything he thought could be improved.

A smile eased over her mouth, because as reluctant as she was about Hoyt getting a moment by moment look at the problems on her small place, there were things she wanted too much with Hoyt to leave to chance.

"I'd be the boss, huh?"

His dark brows went up. "Didn't I say that a couple seconds ago?"

"Just wanted to make sure I heard right."

His gaze narrowed. "Yeah, but you've

got that little smile that says you don't believe it.'' His hand tightened on hers and he gave her a stern look. ''Well, you've just tossed down the gauntlet, Mrs. Donovan, and I'm just the man to pick it up.

Eadie laughed at that. Impressive words, but Hoyt was *always* the boss. It would be quite a challenge for the macho boss of Donovan Ranch to take orders from the lady boss of Webb Ranch. ''I reckon we'll see.''

He leaned over then to give her a hard kiss before he drew back a little. ''Oh, ye of little faith. Are you ready to go?''

''Whenever you are.''

They dropped their cups off in the kitchen on their way out to the pickup. Hoyt briefly drove her around the parts of the headquarters she hadn't seen much of before they headed out through one of the pastures. As soon as they were out of sight of the ranch buildings, Hoyt stopped the pickup and pulled her into his arms for a kiss that easily defeated the vehicle's chilly air-conditioning.

They returned to the house for lunch. After they ate, Hoyt called Reece and found out that little Rachel Gray Waverly had been born at 1:47 that morning. Reece had just returned home after taking his son Bobby to see his new baby sister, and they'd be bringing Leah and the baby home tomorrow afternoon.

Hoyt called the florist himself to order flowers for Leah, and they made plans to visit the baby at Waverly Ranch in a couple of days. That afternoon, they went to Coulter City to shop for a baby gift at the mall, and it touched Eadie to find out that Hoyt had already bought a gift for Bobby so he wouldn't feel left out.

And what a gift it was—a battery-powered car large enough for Bobby to ride in. Not only had Hoyt realized the child might feel a bit left out in the excitement over a new baby, but he'd chosen a wonderful gift for a little boy who was in love with vehicles of any kind.

After supper that night they packed clothes to go to Webb Ranch the next morning. Hoyt meant to take a couple of the horses he usually worked with, and he'd already loaded the tack in the trailer he'd hitched to his pickup.

Their second night together was only a

little less chaste and reserved than their wedding night. They weren't as self-conscious with each other, but that was no huge improvement. Hoyt had pulled her close for a kiss as soon as he'd snapped off the light, but it was brief before he settled her against his side, expelled a gusty breath, and told her good-night.

Eadie couldn't help but feel disappointed. Hoyt was an accomplished flirt and lover, but he didn't seem to be making much effort at either with her. Yes, they'd had more than one toe-curling kiss that day but as the evening had gone on, Hoyt had become more remote. He'd told her last night he couldn't promise not to try to seduce her, but he didn't seem at all interested in doing that now. Not that she wanted to become intimate too soon, but she also didn't want to be the kind of woman he could take or leave.

It seemed very much as if Hoyt was still the hard-to-get and hard-to-keep bachelor he'd always been, despite his plan for them to make a family together and stay married until she planted him in the ground. That part about staying married till death suddenly seemed more like the well-intentioned brag of a man who couldn't begin to follow through with his own plan, much less advance it much beyond speaking a few "I do's" in a church. Did he still mean to?

Though she hoped it was only because he was trying to be considerate of her, Eadie couldn't help but compare the tepid way Hoyt behaved tonight with his initial impatience to marry her and the happiness he'd seemed to have in the week leading up to the wedding. Then there'd been his enthusiasm over everything yesterday. For a man who was as unsubtle and out-with-it as Hoyt was about his feelings, he was simply too cool and contained now for a man with his drive and his level of amorous experience.

And wasn't this the man who'd been so eager to sire heirs that he'd married a woman he didn't love so he could get them? Eadie had assumed he'd meant to do that as soon as possible, considering the recent brush with mortality that had made him worry about dying before he had at least one child to pass on his heritage to.

But there was no hint of worry about him now, and certainly no sense of impatience to conceive a child. Whatever his romantic abilities with women, Hoyt hadn't actually treated her to many of those. Was romancing a girlfriend more exciting for him than romancing a wife? Was the idea of sex not as tantalizing to him now that he was married? Was she simply not as much of a challenge as the unmarried beauties he'd always preferred?

Or was there something about her that didn't much turn him on after all, despite what he'd said about "lighting a short fuse?" He'd remarked just that morning that he'd had to stop their kiss because they might not be able to get out of bed until noon. But it was a fact that there'd been no more remarks like those the rest of the day, not even tonight when a husband's thoughts should have naturally gone to what usually happened between newlyweds at bedtime.

Was she making too much of nothing? Hoyt respected her, and he did have strong feelings about not coming on too strong with her because of what had happened years ago. Instead of worrying about it, she should be grateful he was considerate and so careful not to make her uncomfortable.

She should be rejoicing over the fact that he wasn't pressuring her for sex. On the other hand, it would be a lot more reassuring if he showed some sign of having trouble keeping his hands to himself.

Eadie finally realized how ridiculous her thoughts were becoming, and after a while she was able to stop speculating and go to sleep.

CHAPTER TEN

THEY arrived at Webb Ranch before 8:00 a.m., and drove directly to the barn to unload Hoyt's horses and stow his tack. They turned both horses into one of the corrals and unhitched the trailer. After that, they drove back to the house.

Eadie carried in one of her suitcases and her toiletries case, and took them up to her room while Hoyt brought in their other things from the pickup. She quickly changed the sheets on her bed and put clean towels in the bathroom, then checked to make sure she'd gotten most of her things out of the chest of drawers so Hoyt could put his folded clothes in it. Her things could go in the dresser, which she had yet to completely empty. Last week she'd only had time to move so many things, and she'd have to finish the task in the next days or weeks.

It was just as well this was a hurry-up

job, or she would have dithered endlessly over preparing the bedroom, perhaps moving more things in or out, but certainly moving out a lot of the keepsakes she had accumulated over the years. Hoyt's bedroom was huge compared to hers, and it was masculine and far more elegant, so much so that it could have been photographed for a decorating magazine.

Unlike hers, which still had photos wedged in the frame of the dresser mirror, some that dated back to high school, a couple of Country music posters on the wall from years ago, plus a lifetime of acquired "girl" things, awards and track ribbons from school, along with her favorite teddy bear from childhood.

Her bed was a regular double bed, much smaller than Hoyt's king-sized one, and the handmade quilt on it was far less luxurious than the bedspread on Hoyt's. At least they were developing the habit of sleeping close to each other all night, but Hoyt was so tall she hoped the double mattress would be long enough to accommodate him comfortably.

Hoyt had brought everything else to the top of the back stairs and was just bringing in the garment bag that held their hang-up clothes, when she turned and saw his dark gaze catch sight of the teddy bear that sat on the night table next to the bed. From there, his gaze shot around the room, noting the male Country stars on the posters before it swung back to land on the bed. The measuring look he gave it was quick but unguarded, and Eadie couldn't help her smile as she opened the closet door and he carried the clothes over to hang them on the rod inside.

"Does the mattress look long enough?" she asked as he finished and turned to glance again at the bed.

"I reckon we'll find out. I could hang my feet off the end if I had to." Now he looked at the bear and reached to pick it up and give it a gentle squeeze before he set it down. "Will I have to make room for your little buddy?"

Eadie grinned a little sheepishly. "He usually keeps watch on the table, but he can sleep in the other bedroom this week."

Hoyt glanced around, then walked to the dresser for a closer look at the photos wedged in the frame of the mirror. Too late Eadie remembered there were two newspaper clippings of him taped to the frame. They'd been there so long that she hadn't given them a thought, and she cringed as Hoyt leaned forward a bit more, as if to get a better look. Or to silently draw her attention to the fact that he'd seen them.

Oh my, what should she say? Was it all right for him to find out—or even guess—that she'd adored him for years? And that she'd clipped those pieces because they included fairly good photos as well as news about him?

Considering how remote he'd been—there'd been a warm kiss in bed this morning, but nothing like yesterday—he might not be flattered. He was standing at the right spot in front of the mirror, so she couldn't see his face, and she couldn't help that she moved a little to the side to get a glimpse of his expression.

A faint smile tugged at one corner of his mouth, and there was a glint in his eyes. Humor?

Eadie laced her fingers together and found herself babbling out, "I'd forgotten about those. It's not often a neighbor gets their picture in the paper, unless it's a wedding announcement or an obituary."

"Huh." Hoyt's dark gaze met hers in the mirror. A gleam came into his eyes, a kind of alertness that let her know he'd detected the half-lie the moment she'd spoken. "Reckon not."

He was subtly calling her bluff with his low *Reckon not,* and her hot cheeks went hotter. "I-if we finish bringing things in, we can get started on the outside work."

The faint smile on his mouth widened a fraction, as if he had some secret of his own, and Eadie felt the tide of heat in her cheeks flow down through her body.

"That's a mighty guilty looking blush, Miss Eadie," he drawled as he turned to look at her. "I've rarely seen one that bright."

His voice had gone low and a little rough, and she felt it stroke her insides. They were standing two feet apart, and yet the wild thrill that went through her was the same one she felt when she was pressed against him.

"That's probably not quite the truth," she got out, dismayed at the breathless quality in her voice. "I'm sure you've seen women blush a time or two."

''Let's just say I've never been so flattered by a blush before.''

Her husband was flirting with her. The distance she'd worried about last night and that morning was somehow gone. He looked pleased and Eadie had a hard time suppressing a shy smile as he took a slow step closer.

''I'm putting you on the spot, huh?'' Now he reached up to lightly brush a strand of dark hair from her flushed cheek.

''Yes, you are.''

He grazed her jaw with the back of a knuckle. His gaze was glittering and intense, and her blood began to thicken as her body responded to the hint of seduction. Her instinct was to look down or look away, but she couldn't seem to pull her gaze from the mesmerizing power of his. She couldn't get in a full breath either.

''A man likes to know his wife might have given him a thought or two in the past.'' Now his fingers combed gently into her hair and he leaned down slowly, as if he was giving her time to confess before he kissed her.

His glittering gaze was all but insisting

on that, so she got out a faint, ''I...have had a thought. Or two.''

His low, ''Good,'' was a whisper just before his lips eased tenderly onto hers.

All too soon, he ended it and Eadie opened dazed eyes to his. His voice was gruff.

''I suppose you're gonna remind me again that we've got work to do.''

That was probably about the last thing she would have said to him. The moment he'd turned from the mirror and leveled that gleaming look on her, thoughts about anything but him had flitted away. The smile that came over his mouth in those next quiet seconds was nothing less than arrogant proof that he knew the last thing on her mind now was work. It was also a signal that he intended to savor the macho pride he took in that knowledge.

''It's Monday,'' she finally managed.

''And you're the boss,'' he said. ''I hope you go easy on my first day and don't keep me too late. I just got married a couple days ago.''

''I'll keep it in mind, but we'd better get busy if you don't want to work late.'' Oh, she hated having to say that, but it was true. They couldn't take the day off.

"Yes, ma'am." Hoyt eased away slowly, his dark gaze slipping down the front of her before it leaped back up to pierce hers.

Eadie was trapped in that dark gaze, and literally couldn't move until he'd turned away and walked into the hall to carry in the suitcases he'd brought to the top of the stairs. She still felt flushed and a little dizzy. Her body was already clamoring to stay at the house for the day, and she couldn't recall ever being less in the mood to work.

Once he'd brought in the suitcases and set them unopened on the bed, Hoyt was all business for the rest of the workday. Except for an occasional touch and a good half dozen male glances that lingered here and there, there were no more seductive little moments like that morning in her bedroom.

All in all, they got far more done that day than she'd expected, and certainly more than she could have done alone. They'd moved cattle, doctored a calf that had gotten a nasty kick before they'd returned to the house at one o'clock for the cold lunch they'd brought from Donovan Ranch. Afterward they'd driven out to check tanks, repaired a downed strand of barbed wire they'd spotted while moving cattle, then spent a couple of hours in the tractor shed fooling with the tractor before Hoyt insisted on calling his mechanic to come by and have a look.

The heat of the afternoon and the frustration of the old tractor had nicked Hoyt's temper, and as they wiped grease off their hands, he let some of it out.

"You shoulda had a roll bar put on that a long time ago, Eadie. It's not safe, even if it can be fixed."

The criticism was unexpected, and Eadie glanced at him, a little surprised because his tone was harsh.

"I'm careful."

"Careful isn't enough," he argued. "Freak accidents happen all the time. You work alone too much, you're tired too often. All it takes is some fool thing going wrong, a slope you take too steep or too fast—hell, any number of things—including ones you'd never think of until that tractor was coming down on top of you."

He finished with the grease rag and slapped it irritably on the workbench before he glared at her. "You'll get a roll bar on that thing, or you won't drive it."

Eadie looked down to finish wiping the worst of the dark grease off her hands. Yes, Hoyt was upset, talking tough and barking orders, but she knew his concern was genuine. She was secretly pleased he was so fiery over the idea that she might get hurt.

And he was right. Part of the reason she'd been so careful about where she took the tractor and how she used it was because she knew the danger. She should have had the roll bar put on years ago.

"What? No comment on that?" he persisted. "I mean it, Eadie."

"I know you do," she said patiently as she finished with the rag and looked up at him. "But there's no reason to invest in a three- or four-hundred-dollar roll bar for a tractor that might have to be junked." She could tell he wanted to say more because his mouth was stiff with the effort to keep silent.

He probably wanted to rail around more about safety and to demand to know why she hadn't had a roll bar put on before this, but it was clear he didn't want to put her in a position to mention money troubles. And yet money wasn't the only reason she'd neglected the expense.

"I've had the money in the past to do it," she told him, "but it wasn't the priority it should have been."

"Well, it's a priority now," he declared, and she smiled a little. Hoyt had tried so hard not to be the autocrat he usually was, and he'd managed it most of the day, but he'd clearly reached his limit.

"All right," she said, not troubled over acquiescing, partly because he felt so strongly about it and she should have it done, but mostly because the tractor was probably a nonissue. Hoyt's mechanic was more likely to pronounce it hopeless than to advise an overhaul anyway. Her next tractor—if she kept Webb Ranch—would have all the modern safety features.

Eadie made her smile widen as she tossed the grease rag to the workbench. "How about something cold to drink before we get the stalls ready for your horses and do the late chores?"

Hoyt gave her a narrow look. "Did you

just say you *wouldn't* fight me about that roll bar?''

Eadie shrugged. ''I said 'all right.' I thought it sounded agreeable.''

''You gave in pretty fast.''

She stepped to his side to loop her arm through his and start him walking out of the shed. ''Well, that just shows how reasonable I am.'' Eadie glanced up at him. ''I hope my new husband will be just as reasonable when it's his turn...because no, sorry. I didn't mean I'd *always* give in, but it seemed sensible this time. You were right anyway.''

Hoyt gave a cranky frown. ''You were doing a good job being a submissive little wife—until you spoiled it with that.'' Eadie's brows went up.

''Really? That's exactly what I meant to do, I just wasn't sure you'd get the message. But thanks, Hoyt.'' She gave his arm a pat. ''You're a quick study with this husband thing. I'll probably have you trained by the end of the week.''

The blank surprise on his face made her giggle and she pulled her arm out of his and started briskly ahead. A quick glance over her shoulder told her he'd come to a halt, so she kept walking, listening alertly for the sound of bootsteps behind her.

Instead she heard him growl something, so she burst into a sprint to the house, barely making it to the porch door before Hoyt caught up with her, pulled her to a laughing stop, then kissed her senseless.

He broke off the kiss only long enough to grouse, "I shoulda paid more attention to those track ribbons in your room," before he kissed her again. It took a few minutes to get into the house and even longer to wash up and get something cold to drink.

After that, whatever work discipline either of them had was spotty at best. Yes, they got the stalls ready and made their way through chores, but long looks and longer kisses and a bit of horseplay dragged out the process until they heard Miss Ed drive in and toot her car's horn. They raced through the last couple of things and hurried to the house.

They were just coming in the back door when Miss Ed turned from the counter and gave them a head to toe glance.

"Well, you both need a bath. Do you

wanna wash up and eat it now, or should I leave it to warm in the oven before I head home?''

''We'll wash up and have it now,'' Hoyt told her as Eadie hung her hat on a wall peg next to the door and he followed suit.

''Thanks for bringing supper, Miss Ed,'' Eadie said as she walked to the sink to wash up first so she could take over with the food. ''Are you sure this isn't a big inconvenience?''

''Nah. Since you're cookin' your own breakfast, I'll only be coming over before supper, then I'm done for the day anyway. Now that I don't have anyone at the house, I can catch up with a couple cleaning projects I've been meaning to get at while the boss is out of the way.''

She pushed the reheat button on the microwave and then added, ''I put your lunches for the next couple days in the fridge, and there's notes on 'em about how long they need to heat. A little dessert, too.''

Eadie smiled over at the woman. ''Thanks a million, but if you don't want to bother, just let me know.''

''Won't happen. If there's nothing else

you two need, I'll be gettin' home,'' she said as she reached for her basket. Hoyt picked it up before she could and started toward the door.

''Go on ahead, and thanks again,'' Eadie said as she took the towel off the bar and turned to finish drying her hands as Hoyt opened the door for Miss Ed. ''I'm sorry we weren't at the house to help you bring things in. We'll try to do better tomorrow night.''

Miss Ed waved that away. ''If you're late, it'll be in the oven.'' And then she walked onto the porch, paused while Hoyt reached past her to open the porch door, then went on down the steps to the sidewalk.

He came back in after he'd carried the basket to the car and seen Miss Ed off. Eadie had put another of the dishes in the microwave to heat and was just setting the table.

''Do you think I was too quick about rushing her to her car?'' Hoyt asked as he crossed to the sink to wash up for supper. Eadie smiled.

''Why? Did she say that?''

'''Here's your hat, what's your hurry?'''

he said mimicking Miss Ed's deadpan tone. "Asked if I realized I was stuffing her in the car."

Eadie laughed. "Were you?"

"I thought I was polite about it," he groused. "For a wiry little gal, she was awful slow tonight."

"She was having fun with you."

"Do tell," he said as he finished washing up and dried his hands and forearms. He hung the towel and turned to walk over and pull her into his arms.

"Coming here for the week was a good idea," he declared. "I get you to myself, and I get to find out what you're really like when you're doing everyday things." He leaned down. "And now that those everyday things are done, it's high time we got to doing newlywed things."

He closed that two-inch span between their lips and kissed her.

Hoyt's declaration about doing newlywed things was frustrated by practical things that couldn't wait. After supper, he watched the news while she showered. Eadie was tempted to unpack their suitcases, but left them to give Hoyt his turn in the shower. He looked disapproving when she'd come downstairs in clean jeans and a fresh shirt, as if he suspected she meant to slip into the den to do paperwork.

Once she heard the shower go on upstairs, she raced through the mail and tried to catch up a couple small things, but when Hoyt came in later, he prohibited another moment's work. Eadie got around that by enlisting him to help with the supper dishes. Hoyt did a fair, though awkward job with the dish towel, then, of course, boasted that he hadn't broken anything as she smiled and prepared the coffeemaker and set the timer for morning.

After Eadie finished wiping down the table and the counter, Hoyt's plan to relax in the living room was delayed when she reminded him they hadn't finished unpacking. Though he likely considered that another female task, he went upstairs with her and gamely set about moving his clothes into the chest of drawers.

Eadie managed hers swiftly, then turned in time to see Hoyt carelessly cramming rolls of socks and underwear in the same drawer he'd put jeans and work shirts in. She walked over to intervene.

"Let me take care of those," she said, secretly pleased to do a wifely thing for him. "There are plenty of empty drawers."

Hoyt moved aside and looked on as she sorted the jumble of socks and underwear into a separate drawer, straightened the work shirts in the drawer he'd been using, then switched his folded jeans into a lower, deeper drawer. He added more things to appropriate drawers.

"Now you know for sure I don't have any housekeeping skills," he said as she finished and closed the drawers.

"It's not too late to learn," she pointed out as she turned and walked to the bed to close and latch the suitcases.

"I might get around to learning a few if you and Miss Ed didn't take over and do them for me at the first sign of male innovation," he complained as he took the suitcases and set them out of the way on the floor.

"So that's what it's called," Eadie said then laughed. "I let you dry dishes."

"Yeah, you did, but when do I get to wash?"

Eadie shook her head. "Aren't you afraid the story will get around? What about your chauvinist image?'' Hoyt stepped closer and caught her waist.

''What chauvinist image? The day I let you drive me around Coulter City in my new pickup was the day I proved I didn't have a chauvinist bone in my body.''

''Hah,'' she scoffed, trying for humor as she lifted her hands to his chest. Her heart was fluttering at the look in his eyes, and her knees felt a little weak. ''You wouldn't want to chance showing up somewhere with dishpan hands.''

Hoyt rolled his eyes. ''It'll never go *that* far, darlin','' he said as he pulled her against him and her body went a little wild.

Her hands had gone up his shirtfront and her arms had automatically wrapped around his neck as if they'd done this for years. Something had changed between them today, and this was another confirmation of the new closeness between them. Eadie suddenly knew tonight wouldn't be as chaste as the past two nights, and her insides shivered with both excitement and nerves.

As if to confirm her intuition, Hoyt's gruff, ''When's bedtime around here?''

was all but a formal announcement. Eadie tried to sound casual about it.

"Did I wear you out today?"

His handsome mouth tilted into a sexy half smile. "I've still got some spark in my engine. How 'bout you?"

A tide of shyness swept through her, and she felt the heat in her face.

"I'm not sure I'd put it quite that way, but I'm okay."

Hoyt chuckled, then leaned down until his lips eased against hers.

CHAPTER ELEVEN

IT WAS a tender kiss, one that was tentative yet searching, as if the care Hoyt took was because he wanted more but wasn't about to rush a response from her that she didn't want to give.

The emotion that welled up at the realization combined with the lazy expertise he treated her to and Eadie couldn't have held back a response if her life had depended on it. Hoyt followed her lead for only a few seconds before he took over.

The kiss went so scorching and deep that her knees failed. She stayed upright only because his strong arms took her weight. A cyclone of sensation spiraled up, and whatever reserve she had evaporated.

As strongly as she'd reacted to Hoyt's kisses in the past few days, it was nothing compared to her reaction now. Her feet weren't even touching the floor anymore.

The room was spinning, or rather they

were, and the next thing she knew Hoyt was lowering her to the bed. He followed her down, his big body barely breaking full contact with hers before he was lying half over her. Eadie couldn't get enough of what his mouth was doing and urged him on, clinging to him, clutching him, shivering with delight when his free hand roamed over her with matching fervor.

He finally broke off the kiss to take in a quick breath before he eased down to press his lips to the side of her throat. She sighed at the sharp excitement when he went lower, and didn't realize until his lips made their way to the sensitized skin just above her bra that he'd somehow unbuttoned several buttons of her blouse.

A huge tremor went through him and he suddenly stopped. Eadie realized she'd been alternately clutching at his wide shoulders and running her fingers through his thick hair. She still was, so consumed with the utter joy of how it felt to indulge herself like this that she hadn't been able to resist.

The fact that he'd stopped what he was doing and now held himself so rigidly began to get through to her. A second later, she realized her hands had shifted to the back of his shirt, gripping it as if she was either desperate to keep hold of him or trying to rip it off. Hoyt's voice was half rasp, half groan.

"Ah, Eadie..."

Another tremor went through him and it dawned on her that Hoyt was so stirred up his big body was all but shaking with desire. For her. His warm mouth moved back onto her skin for another voracious kiss, as if he couldn't help himself. Hoyt was a big man, a strong one, so it was out of character for him to tremble. The fact that he did now—and with her—made her feel desirable and amazingly powerful.

"Eadie?"

She couldn't mistake the real question behind the one he spoke against her skin. He was asking for more, much more. His iron tension told her he was already at the point of no return, and yet he was trying to hold back for her sake, fighting the demands of his own body.

The battle was less intense for her. Excitement, arousal, and the fierce craving for more of him and more of this had arrowed past her every reservation. Every sensible ideal she'd had about waiting for a love declaration suddenly didn't seem quite as important as what her body was so on fire to have.

"It's...all right." Eadie's strained whisper was nearly a plea.

"You're sure?"

The hoarse words sent a fresh rush of emotion through her that was stronger than whatever nervousness remained. Hoyt was her husband and he cared for her. She hoped he didn't expect perfection from her tonight, but he already knew she was inexperienced.

And, despite his bluster, Hoyt was a very kind man. He'd promised to be tender with her, and she trusted him for that. And she loved him so much that it almost didn't matter if she had to wait for his feelings for her to grow into more than friendship and liking. Especially when his body trembled again and she felt her insides quiver in response.

"I'm...sure," she got out and Hoyt's mouth found hers for a kiss that banished whatever second thoughts she might have had.

Eadie was distantly aware that Hoyt tried

to go slow, but once she realized even more how a kiss or a soft sound or a daring touch from her interfered with his control, she suddenly couldn't keep herself from taking advantage of it.

Clothing magically disappeared, the quilt and top sheet were shoved aside, and bodies that had begun separately came together in a unity that was as profoundly emotional as it was intensely physical. The small bit of discomfort she felt was quick but just as quickly forgotten.

Eadie was certain she couldn't possibly survive the staggering pleasure of it all as Hoyt took her with him to some soaring place of sensation that took her breath away. They seemed to hover in that golden place of wonder for a few seconds before the pleasure abruptly zoomed even higher. Afterward they sank down into a soft, safe place where they lay in weak silence while their breath slowly came back.

Eadie was so dazed by it all, so awed and drowsy from the pleasure that still pulsed through her that she couldn't move. But then, she didn't want to move, not even an eyelash. The feel of Hoyt's hot body on hers was heavy, satisfyingly heavy. And wonderful. He was hers, she thought dreamily, now and forever.

When she woke up later, it was almost 2:00 a.m. Hoyt had shifted his weight off her, but they were wrapped snugly together face-to-face beneath the covers. The heat of his body seemed to ignite hers, and she felt a ripple of desire go through her that made her press closer.

Though Hoyt was deeply asleep, his arms tightened around her a moment, but then slowly relaxed, and she lay in the dark a while, savoring the wonder of what they'd done, hoping it had been as wonderful for Hoyt. Surely he couldn't have made her feel like that if he hadn't been motivated at least a tiny bit by love. Could he?

And was he really so experienced that he could have shared what they'd had with just any woman? Had it been as special for him as it had been for her, as emotional?

Though he'd seemed to be as affected as she'd been, surely she was too much a novice to have driven him as wild as he had her, and it was only inexperience that made her blind to any hint that what they'd done had been only ‘‘the usual’’ or ‘‘so-so’’ for him.

Well, if things had been only ‘‘the usual’’ or ‘‘so-so’’ for him, she’d do better next time. Or the next. Whether or not she’d pleased him as much as she’d hoped, it was wonderfully reassuring that he held her so close in his sleep, as if she was precious to him, as if he didn’t want even an inch of space between them.

Eadie decided to be happy with that.

The next time Eadie awoke, it was morning, and neither of them had moved. Though it was still dark in the bedroom, the inky sky outside the window was going lighter.

The last thing she wanted was to move away from Hoyt, but shyness made her leery of her new husband seeing her nakedness. Yes he’d seen her last night, but getting out of bed to put on the robe she’d hung in the bathroom was something she preferred to do while the room was dark and Hoyt was still asleep.

Though Eadie considered her body to be work-toned and fit and not lacking in feminine attributes, she still wasn’t eager to call attention to the differences between her and the women who'd had either the vanity to keep their pampered bodies perfect or the money to make them perfect. On top of that, simple modesty wouldn't allow her to just parade around without clothes after only one night of intimacy. She just wasn't wired that way.

It was a small challenge to unwrap herself from Hoyt's arms without waking him, since he was just as accustomed to rising before dawn as she was. She managed it and had moved away enough to slip from under the top sheet and quilt to stand when she heard him chuckle behind her.

"Lucky for me, I've got good night vision, darlin'," he rasped, his low voice rusty from sleep, "though you might be surprised how well that cute little backside shows up in the early light."

Eadie managed not to dive for cover as Hoyt chuckled again, the lazy male sound both relaxed and amused. Thank heavens he couldn't see the bashful smile that mortification had sent up, or the fierce blush that seemed to sting her skin from scalp to toes as she walked to the bathroom and shut herself in.

She'd meant to get her robe and go downstairs to bring up their coffee before she had a quick shower, but she'd heard the lamp in the bedroom snap on just before she'd closed the door. She might as well get the shower out of the way—it would give her time to recover—but then she was assailed by a fit of giggles over Hoyt's orneriness. At least in here the sound of running water covered them.

In moments she was out and dried off, tying the robe's belt, taking a moment to glance into the mirror to brush her hair and make certain she looked cool and composed, but struck by the subtle differences in her face. Yes, there was still a trace of puffiness in her lips, but it was her eyes that seemed different, more worldly. The fact that her hair was more tousled than usual and required extra brushing was a reminder that Hoyt's hands had mussed it up.

And remembering how that had felt brought back the memories—and almost the sensations—of how the other things he'd done had felt. Now the new gleam in her eyes that made them seem so deep and blue seemed to have a definition, one that was part feminine satisfaction and part feminine desire for more.

Would Hoyt be able to tell? Had what they'd done last night forever stripped her of the ability to keep her feelings from him? In truth, the only thing that motivated her to keep anything from him now was pride. There'd been no love words from either of them, at least none from him. She was a little hazy on things she might have said because she'd been so swept away, but she was fairly certain she'd kept that secret. At least she couldn't recall Hoyt showing any reaction, good or bad, if she had said something like "I love you."

His low voice coming from the other side of the closed door startled her a little.

"I've got your coffee, Mrs. Donovan. Come have a sip and kiss me." He paused. "Or kiss me and have a sip. This cup and I can't wait another second for some attention."

Hoyt's playfulness sent a fresh wave of emotion crashing through her that gripped her throat and stung her eyes. She loved him so much it hurt, and it took everything she had to compose herself.

Oh, how she wanted to tell him, to confess it all, but the thought that she could spoil things between them by speaking too soon terrified her. Hoyt liked her and cared about her, but he'd married her to have children, not because he was in love with her. The last thing she wanted to do was scare him off or, almost as bad, make him feel obligated to say "I love you," if the words weren't from his heart.

Eadie took a steadying breath and opened the door, managing to smile, then almost laughing when she saw that Hoyt's eyes were closed, and he'd bent down, his mouth fixed in readiness for a kiss. He held the cup next to his beard rough jaw as if offering her the choice he'd mentioned, and he'd put on a pair of jeans, though from the telltale peep of bare skin behind the open button, jeans were all he had on. Eadie took the cup at the same instant she gave him a quick kiss.

"How's that?" she asked as she drew back and sipped the coffee. Hoyt opened his eyes to give her a grumpy look.

"Aw, you're a tough one, Eadie. Won't even toss me a crumb, and now I'll wonder all day if you picked me first or the coffee."

Eadie didn't take that seriously. It was just another little flirtation.

"Poor baby. And I kissed you before I had the sip."

"Yeah, but only 'cause you couldn't get the cup to your..." his dark gaze dropped suggestively to her mouth, "lips first."

"A meaningless technicality," she said, then reached up to pull him down for a slower, nicer kiss.

Hoyt lifted his head only long enough to growl, "Now that's more like it," before he kissed her again.

Eadie forgot about her coffee until Hoyt jerked his head up and drew back to catch her hand and level the cup.

Eadie looked to see what the problem was, saw the spots of coffee on his bare toes, then giggled. "Oops. Sorry."

"Yeah, oops. When's breakfast around here?"

"As soon as you let me get dressed and go downstairs."

"Huh. Well, I guess you'd better go before you scald the hide off my feet."

Eadie smiled up at him. "I guess."

"You guess," he growled, then gave her a swift, hard kiss before he let her go.

Eadie stepped past him and set her coffee down to get out clothes for the day and find a hair tie. When the bathroom door clicked shut, she took her things into the other bedroom and got dressed. She took a moment to go back in and make the bed while she listened to the novel sound of an electric shaver behind the closed bathroom door. By the time it went off, she was headed downstairs.

‘‘How ’bout we make plans to go see that new baby tonight?’’ Hoyt said as they were finishing breakfast.

‘‘We’d probably better call first and see if Leah’s up to company,’’ Eadie cautioned. Hoyt dismissed that.

‘‘If Leah’s out of the hospital, she oughta be ready for company.’’

Eadie’s brows went up. ‘‘You don’t know much about postpartum, do you? Just because she’s out of the hospital doesn’t mean she’s ready for much beyond resting and taking care of the baby. And then there’s Bobby, who needs her attention, too.’’

Hoyt frowned. ‘‘It’s too early to throw around fancy words. Post-what?’’

Eadie smiled. "Postpartum is the time after birth. You'll find out more about that as we go along. Let's just say Leah will have to take it easy for a while, even if Reece did get a housekeeper."

"You know about that kind of woman and baby stuff?"

"I know a few things, and not much about those."

"Maybe we ought to buy some books so you can read up on 'em," he said, and it was typical that he'd assign that task to the female half of the equation, as if he was too macho to learn much about it himself. "Never know when something like that might come in handy."

He was grinning by the time he added that last part, his dark eyes glittering. He was making light of it, but it was a reminder of his reason for marrying her that made her more determined than ever not to say a word about love unless he did.

And she also resolved not to be disheartened about that, just...patient. Keeping silent was already harder to do than she'd ever dreamed, but at the moment, patience seemed impossible.

* * *

They managed to get through the work well enough to finish up chores before Miss Ed arrived with supper. Since Reece had told Hoyt that day that Leah was looking forward to showing off little Rachel tonight, they planned to have time to shower before supper so they could get the dishes out of the way and stop by Donovan Ranch to pick up the gifts they'd bought for the baby and Bobby.

Miss Ed brought a few phone messages with supper, and was soon on her way. After they ate, they did the dishes and while Hoyt returned a phone call that couldn't wait, Eadie changed into a summer dress and grabbed her handbag before she rejoined him.

It had been a good day. Hoyt had been mostly business while they'd been working, but not only was he flirtatious and frequently affectionate when they were at the house, he was good company all the time. They did indeed get along well, though Eadie sensed more and more that he was looking for a way around her pride to somehow help her hang on to Webb Ranch. Today he'd asked about her wells and remarked that the highway fence needed some work.

Which they both knew was a polite way to say the fence really ought to be replaced. And that was just one more thing that she'd made do with while she tried to make up her mind about what to do with the ranch.

When they arrived at Waverly Ranch, Bobby came racing out the front door to meet them, and Hoyt gave Eadie a wink before he handed the boy the gaily wrapped baby gift and sent him ahead of them into the house to give it to his mother. The little boy was happy to do so, and once he was out of sight, Hoyt quickly flipped the tarp off the motorized ride-on car in the truck bed and lifted it out.

Eadie waited outside the front door while Hoyt went around the house to set the toy on the back patio before he rejoined her and they walked into the open front door just in time for Reece to come into the entry hall.

"I wondered what was keeping you," he said.

Hoyt took off his Stetson and upended it on the entry table. "Just sneakin' a little surprise out back, but that's for later. Where's that baby girl?''

''Getting her diaper changed for company,'' Reece answered, then greeted Eadie. ''Hey there, Eadie. You're so pretty tonight I don't have to ask how the marriage is going.''

''Thanks. How's Leah?''

''Looking forward to company. Come on in and sit down,'' Reece said.

They walked into the living room and Reece offered them iced tea that they declined until later. The pink sweetheart roses Hoyt had sent Leah at the hospital were on the coffee table, and they were gorgeous. Eadie sat on the sofa, but Bobby came racing in to fling himself at Hoyt before he could sit down.

Hoyt caught him and tossed him into the air. ''Hey there, big brother. What have you been up to?''

''Helpin' Momma with my baby sister. Babies can't play much,'' Bobby chirped with happy candor as Hoyt held him suspended in the air. ''An' she stinks.''

Hoyt feigned a look of horror and abruptly lowered the boy so they were face-to-face. "Ah, no. Should we trade her for a sister who smells better?"

"*Noooo,*" Bobby laughed, then shrieked when Hoyt gave him another toss into the air.

"Where'd you put the present, squirt?"

"Momma's got it. She says it's too pretty to open."

"Well, ain't that just like a woman?" Hoyt sent Eadie a sparkling glance, then turned Bobby so he was facing her. "Say hello to your aunt Eadie."

Bobby gave her his attention, and Eadie smiled. "Hi, Bobby."

"Hi." Now the boy turned bashful, but Hoyt gave him a tickle that made him squeal with delight.

Eadie loved that "Uncle" Hoyt referred to her as "Aunt" Eadie. She approved of the old-fashioned notion that it was improper for a child to address an adult only by their first name, so she'd expected Hoyt to do the usual and refer to her as Miss Eadie. But calling her "Aunt" conferred a family designation, and it underscored the fact that they were officially a couple.

Reece spoke from the doorway. "Wind

him up too much, and we'll send him home with you,'' he warned.

''Killjoy.'' Hoyt stopped the horseplay and sat down next to Eadie with the boy in his lap as Reece carried the baby in with Leah at his side. ''You'd have a fit if we did take him with us.''

''Yeah, 'cause you'd spoil him rotten,'' Reece declared.

Leah looked happy and relaxed, and beautiful. Her cheeks were flushed with healthy color, her loose-fitting cotton sundress no doubt chosen for comfort.

They answered her soft ''Hello,'' with their own.

''Which one of you wants her first?'' Reece asked as Leah sat down on the sofa opposite theirs and he came their way with the baby.

Hoyt spoke up. ''Probably Eadie. I've got my hands full with the squirt.''

Eadie knew instantly that Hoyt had declined so he wouldn't make Bobby feel pushed aside for the baby. It was a pretty sensitive thing to do. After all, Hoyt had grown up an only child, as she had, so neither of them had a first hand experience with sibling rivalry. It pleased her that Hoyt had known about it anyway.

Reece bent down to place little Rachel in her arms. Though she'd held a baby from time to time, Eadie had never held one this tiny. Rachel had lots of dark hair. Her little eyes were open, and they fixed on Eadie's face right away.

"Oh, she's perfect...gorgeous," Eadie said softly, then gently opened a bit of the light blanket the baby was wrapped in to get a better look at the frilly pink and white dress that looked almost small enough to fit one of her old dolls.

The scent of baby powder that wafted up was easily the sweetest smell on earth. Rachel was so warm and cuddly and precious that Eadie held her even closer. One little hand moved out of a fold of blanket, and Eadie marveled at the tiny, elegant fingers that were open, then slowly curled into a fist before her rosebud mouth opened in a yawn that was darling.

"No, no, don't go to sleep yet, pretty girl," Eadie crooned as she draped the blanket closed, leaving the baby's hand out as she gently stroked a satiny cheek with her fingertip.

Bobby was crowding close to look on and reached out.

"She likes to hold my finger. See?" he asked as Rachel latched on to his finger, though she was still staring at Eadie.

Hoyt leaned around Bobby. "She's not much bigger than a minute," he said, careful to keep his voice low. "And look at those eyes. They've still got that fresh-from-heaven shine."

Eadie glanced at Hoyt, touched by his hushed, almost reverent tone as he looked at the baby. The whimsy about Rachel's eyes having a "fresh-from-heaven shine" got her by the heart. She suddenly loved him so much that she was bursting with it.

Hoyt's gaze lifted to Eadie's and when she saw the gleam in his eyes, she remembered what he'd said the day they were married.

I'd like about a half dozen like that little one…and at least six of the other kind.

After her protest, he'd amended it to *however many you want to give after two of each.*

Now that she was holding Rachel and had fallen in love with her, the idea of having a dozen children wasn't quite so appalling. Not that she seriously wanted a dozen, but she was suddenly eager to get started and no longer cared how high the count went.

Eadie saw that same eagerness in Hoyt's dark eyes and instantly knew he'd be even more impatient to produce heirs. She also became aware that Reece and Leah were watching the silent byplay between them, so she broke contact with Hoyt's gaze and glanced over at Leah.

"How are you feeling?"

"Tired, but surprisingly good. I might not be able to say that if Reece hadn't insisted on hiring a housekeeper to take care of everything else for a few weeks. I love taking care of my own house, but it'll be nice to only have Bobby and Rachel to take care of for a while."

Reece leaned close to his wife. "You know I'd like to make that arrangement permanent. In the meantime, you're gonna let the rest of us help with Bobby. You'll have plenty of time to chase after him when you get your strength back."

Leah smiled serenely. "Yes, boss." Then after she thanked them for the roses, she said to Bobby, ''Why don't you come sit with Momma?''

Bobby left his sister to sit with his mother on the other sofa, giving her a kiss before he snuggled against her side. Reece had his arm around Leah and he rested his hand on the boy's head. Eadie felt envious of the loving picture they made, but when the baby made a restless move, she looked back down into the bright eyes that were still staring calmly up at her.

CHAPTER TWELVE

THEY talked about babies, Bobby in particular, and Eadie happily listened to the other three adults. The longtime closeness between them was obvious, and she felt fortunate that Reece and Leah had so easily included her in that closeness. Eadie gave Hoyt a turn holding Rachel, who seemed even more fascinated with him than she'd been with Eadie.

In the meantime, Hoyt suggested that Bobby bring the baby gift in to his mother so she could open it. Leah shared the unwrapping with Bobby, then allowed him to open the box that held three beautiful little dresses in different sizes.

They talked a little more before Hoyt changed the subject to glance meaningfully at Reece. "We'd better get to what Aunt Eadie and I brought."

"I reckon," Reece said then stood up.

Hoyt did, too, still holding the baby before he paused and looked over at Leah.

"Do you feel like going out to the kitchen to watch, Miss Leah?"

Leah barely had time to nod before Bobby piped up, "Watch what, Uncle Hoyt?"

"You'll know soon enough, son," Reece said as he helped Leah to her feet. Hoyt waited for Eadie to stand before he handed her the baby.

Bobby started for the kitchen but Hoyt intercepted him and swung him up to tuck him under his arm like a football.

"You're almost too big to carry like this," he teased. "Won't be long before your daddy and I'll have to figure out some other way to tote you around."

The boy giggled gleefully as they all walked to the kitchen with the women leading the way. Reece had followed carrying a wing chair from the living room and he set it in the kitchen next to the glass patio doors before he took a moment to make sure Leah was settled in it comfortably. Hoyt hooked one of the kitchen chairs on his way past the table to set it next to

Leah's for Eadie. Reece stopped just as he started to slide the glass panel open.

"Hold on, Hoyt. We've been using the video camera today, and this might be a good thing to add."

They all waited while Reece went to get the camera. When he came back, the men took the squirming boy outside. Hoyt set Bobby on his feet and bent down to point him toward a tree at the side of the patio where the surprise was parked.

Reece had gone ahead to aim the lens, so he caught it all when Bobby gave a boyish shout and ran to the ride-on toy. As Reece closed in with the camera, the child scrambled into the driver's seat and happily turned the steering wheel before Hoyt showed him how to switch on the motor.

From there, it was all out comedy as Hoyt tried to prevent the miniature car from running down flowers and crashing into the wooden swing while Reece kept ahead of them to film it. Eadie and Leah laughed at the sight of the two tough guys and the small, shrieking driver, who was too excited to pay attention to Hoyt's efforts to coach him on how to coordinate speed with steering.

Finally Hoyt got the car to the far end of the patio where there were fewer obstacles, then had to keep moving to stay with the little car and the pint-size driver who now looked determined to drive to San Antonio.

''We'll never get him to bed tonight,'' Leah said, laughing, ''but it'll be worth every minute. What a wonderful gift.''

By the time they came in, baby Rachel was asleep and Leah was looking tired. Reece took one look and declared that it was bedtime for the two of them. Hoyt seconded that by declaring it was bedtime for everyone. They said their goodbyes and the Waverly's again gave their thanks for the gifts and flowers before Eadie and Hoyt left to give the veteran father a chance to get his family settled for the night.

Eadie was mightily impressed with that. It was obvious that Reece adored Leah. And there was something about a tough, macho man who could take care of a new baby, a toddler and a tired wife, that got to her. Though Hoyt was just as macho as Reece, she knew he'd be able to do the same or would learn to, particularly since he loved children and was so good with them.

As she'd seen that night years ago then again the night he'd brought supper and served it to her, Hoyt would be more than capable of taking care of his own children and tired wife when his time came. Eadie was proud of him for that. It was all she could do not to lean across the seat to kiss him.

Instead she buckled her seat belt. A moment or so later, she sensed Hoyt's mood had turned quiet, but there was a surprising grimness in his profile that got her attention.

It didn't take long to get back to Webb Ranch. Hoyt parked the truck and they walked to the barn for a last look around before they went back to the house. It was a fairly regular habit for Eadie, and since Hoyt's horses were a new addition among hers, it was just better to check things a final time, especially since they'd been away for the evening.

Once they were in the house, Eadie prepared the coffee for morning and set the timer on the coffeemaker while Hoyt checked for messages on her voice mail.

After that, they turned off the lights and went upstairs.

It had been a long day and now that it was full dark and they'd gotten home later than they'd meant to, they were both quiet, though Hoyt's silence still seemed more significant than simple tiredness. In truth, she'd been looking forward to being alone with him tonight. Last night had been wonderful, and it had been hard to keep her distance that day. She was still a little nervous about intimacy, but she couldn't help a very feminine craving for more.

Hoyt pried his boots off on the bootjack by the closet door as if he was still vaguely distracted by his thoughts. Since it was late and she was still shy about undressing in front of him, Eadie walked on into the bathroom and closed the door for privacy. Once she'd changed out of her clothes into her nightgown and robe and took care of necessity, she opened the door and started to remove her light makeup.

Hoyt walked over and leaned against the bathroom door frame to watch the process and she was encouraged by that.

"Do you think we made a baby last

night?'' he asked, and she smiled to cover a mix of feelings.

''I don't think so.''

''Think we'll make one tonight?''

Eadie gave her head a faint shake. Though an hour ago she'd been thrilled by little Rachel and looking forward to having a baby, Eadie's heart fell a little at Hoyt's apparent eagerness to know if they'd conceived a child or if they might tonight. It was another reminder that this marriage was about heirs, not about love, however much they liked each other.

In spite of their ''deal,'' she so wanted Hoyt to be in love with her before they conceived a child, even more now that she'd held a baby who'd so obviously been the product of her parents' love for each other. She would have never married him if she hadn't loved him so much. And frankly, after spending time with the Waverlys, she believed even more that children were especially blessed if they had a mother and father who loved each other as much as Reece and Leah seemed to.

Recalling how her mother and father had been when she was growing up strengthened that belief. Their love for each other had included her, binding the three of them together even more closely than blood, and Eadie wanted that for her children. Though the worst of the hurt of losing her parents had passed, she was suddenly sentimental over her memories of them.

"Something wrong?"

Hoyt's low voice carried a thread of concern that pulled her out of her thoughts but made her hesitant to answer. What could she tell him that wouldn't somehow obligate him to make a love declaration he might not feel? No matter how badly she wanted to hear the words, she could live without them for the rest of her life if she had to, though her heart quivered with hurt at the idea.

Eadie made herself smile at Hoyt's reflection as she finished rinsing off the last of the facial soap with a washcloth. "I was just thinking about my momma and daddy. Reece and Leah reminded me a lot of them tonight."

"Were they as crazy about each other?" he asked, allowing her change of subject, and Eadie had to glance away from the sudden intensity in his dark eyes, using the excuse of rinsing out the washcloth.

"Yes." She mentally raced to think of something to add to keep this subject going as she hung the washcloth on the towel bar before she turned toward him.

"What about your parents?" she asked, striving for a conversational tone. "I never knew much about them. From what I remember, they were older than mine and, of course, they didn't run in the same circles socially."

Hoyt turned somber again, and she felt a nettle of regret because her question must have caused it. Did this have something to do with what he'd been brooding about?

"I was a late baby after years of trying," he told her. "Any differences they had were already settled by the time I came along. There was respect and affection, but I never heard a lot of words about it before Momma died. After she was gone, Daddy took it hard, so hard I thought he'd never come out of it. He did though, but he was never like before. And then he only lasted a year or so after that."

"I'm sorry," Eadie said as she stepped toward him and touched his arm in silent sympathy before he eased away from the door frame and turned to let her pass, managing to slip his arm away from her fingers. Whether that was because he was deflecting her gesture or simply turning to let her pass, she couldn't tell. He followed her out into the bedroom so Eadie told him the part of her story that was similar to his as she walked to her side of the bed.

"Momma threw herself into work after Daddy passed away. At first, I couldn't get her to eat and she couldn't sleep, so we had to get something from the doctor to help with that. I was afraid she'd work herself to death, but work seemed to help the most. Then one day she started getting better."

Eadie shrugged, still not certain there was any one thing that had triggered her mother's improvement except time. "She'd even thought about dating a man she'd gone to high school with, but then she had the wreck."

She turned down the quilt and top sheet before she straightened and looked at Hoyt. He'd stopped a couple of feet away, his fingers wedged in his front jeans' pockets, still somber. His nearness now gave her a quivery feeling of anticipation, but he seemed in the mood to talk.

"Do you ever worry about loving someone that much?'' he asked solemnly. "So much it might kill you if something happened to them?''

Eadie was stunned by the question, instantly sensing the significance of it. Had Hoyt somehow connected loving someone too much with his father's decline after his mother's death? Was that why Hoyt had dated so many women? Even worse, was that why he'd married a woman he didn't love?

Could the shock of his father's death and the trauma of a sudden avalanche of responsibility have compounded the notion that love was something better avoided? Eadie wasn't sure what he was really asking. And she couldn't guess why he'd bring it up now unless it was to maybe explain why he couldn't love her. Oh, she hoped that wasn't it!

Do you ever worry about loving someone that much...so much it might kill you if something happened to them?

Was Hoyt truly worried about that? Had he closed his heart to the possibility? Was that the real reason he'd chosen her, because there was no danger of ever falling in love with her?

Though it hurt to think Hoyt might never allow himself to love any woman, even his wife, Eadie suddenly felt sadder for him than she felt for herself. Now she knew how to answer him.

"I think it would be worse to be crazy about someone who wasn't crazy about you," she finally said, unable to look away from his face. Hoyt was so rarely like this that she couldn't help her growing unease. She almost wished they'd stuck to the subject of babies, anything to keep things from going this dark between them.

She slipped the robe off and tossed it across the foot of the bed, painfully aware that his gaze was fixed on her like a laser. She was suddenly too cowardly to look him in the eye.

"Well, if you don't mind, I'm going to bed," she said, trying to sound casual about it, but Hoyt's low words stopped her.

"You're right."

The silent turbulence coming from him gripped her and she glanced his way.

"You're right, Eadie," he repeated. "As hard as it would be to lose someone you're crazy about, it's worse to be crazy about someone who isn't crazy about you. Or tries to hide it, if they are.''

He spoke as if he'd experienced that, and her heart leaped with excitement. Her first thought was that he was speaking for himself about her. After all, she'd kept her real feelings to herself, and he'd said more than once that she'd kept him guessing, so it was reasonable to think he might be hinting he was in love with her.

But then she remembered Celeste, the first woman in all of Hoyt Donovan's known romantic history to ever have jilted him. Her next thought truly sickened her.

Had he asked about the possibility of making a baby last night because he was looking for a last moment escape from their marriage? Pregnancy would complicate any change of mind he might be having, so maybe the first thing he'd wanted to establish was whether it had happened yet or not.

Once that awful thought had occurred to her, she remembered her inexperience last night. And Hoyt had lost interest in other women so fast. Compared to them, what could Eadie Webb possibly have that would keep him from losing interest in her just as quick? Even as quick as a mere four days of married life?

Yes, Hoyt was a man of his word and he'd married her believing he could hold out till death. But the fact was, he didn't love her. Maybe that's why he'd been so silent and remote since they'd left the Waverly's.

Eadie was suddenly weary of worrying about it, weary of having her heart dragged from worry to hope then back to worry. Maybe it was time to stop wondering, stop speculating. If they'd made a mistake, they needed to acknowledge it. Once they did, they could decide what to do about it, though Eadie was terrified that what might have to be done would be devastating.

Somehow she scraped up the courage to speak, and though she was calm and reasonably cool about it, her voice was barely audible.

"I'm not sure what you're getting at."

His expression went grim. "You honestly can't guess?"

Eadie laced her fingers together as if desperate to hold herself together. "To tell the truth, I'd rather hear you say whatever you mean straight out. Then we'll both be sure we understand each other."

She couldn't help that she held her breath. Hoyt's expression darkened and his brows lowered ominously. She stared, wondering why he suddenly seemed angry. Surely anger wouldn't be part of this?

"All right, dammit, you asked for it," he grumbled as he pulled his fingers out of his pockets, "so now I'm gonna say it straight out."

But then he stopped, as if he was trying to hold back harsh words. He did care about her, so it was natural that he wouldn't want to hurt her feelings. What clearer signal did she need that Hoyt meant to end this? Her heart squeezed with pain and she braced herself for the words he suddenly seemed reluctant to speak.

When he went on, she literally couldn't comprehend his words at first.

"Do you think you'll ever have any kind of feelings for me in even a *mildly* 'crazy' range? Have I got *any* reason to hope for something more than friendship from you, and passion and maybe even love?"

Eadie's mouth dropped open as she mentally grappled with that. ''What did you say?''

Hoyt's frown deepened and he growled, ''You heard me.''

''Do you...hope for something like that? From me?''

Though she'd craved it for a long time, it didn't seem possible for this to be happening so soon, but her heart was going wild with the certainty that it was happening. Finally.

''Not *something* like that,'' he declared. *''That.''*

''That.''

Obviously they were both trying to protect their pride, and Eadie couldn't help the hysterical bubble of laughter that suddenly burst up at how ridiculous they sounded. She only barely managed to keep it back, though Hoyt could apparently tell it was there because he got a cranky look.

''That,'' he said tersely. ''Love.'' He expelled a frustrated breath. ''Do you think,'' he repeated more slowly, ''you'll ever have feelings like that? Something even mildly crazy? A kid oughta have a momma and a daddy who are crazy about each other, don't you think? Otherwise, they're cheated.''

Eadie's eyes were stinging with love and gratitude and rising joy, and she had to blink to keep her vision clear enough to keep watching his face.

''I agree with that completely,'' she said. ''Are you…saying *you* might have a mild case of…crazy?''

Hoyt reached for her hands and glared down at her.

''It's no *mild* case,'' he groused before his dark eyes softened and his voice gentled to a rasp. ''I'm in love with you, Eadie, and have been for a long time. Is that all right with you?''

Joy rushed through her, and a half-choked ''Yes'' came out on a pent up breath. She couldn't have kept the rest of it back if her life had depended on it. ''I've been in love with you for so long, Hoyt, so long.''

Hoyt suddenly caught her up and branded her lips with a fiery kiss that couldn't possibly last long enough. Her arms instantly locked around his neck and Hoyt sat down on the edge of the bed with her in his lap. When he finally broke off the kiss, he drew back to study her flushed face.

"You've been in love with me a long time, huh? How long?"

Eadie was still so full of joy and still so affected by his kiss that the answer slipped out.

"Since the night you came to my rescue."

Hoyt got a pained look. "Ah, Eadie, don't tell me that." She sobered a little to stare at him.

"What's wrong?"

His dark brows curved into cranky whorls. "You tell me you've been in love with me for what, five years? And then I'd have to tell you that I've been in love with you just about that long."

Eadie grinned with foolish glee. "Have you been?" Hoyt frowned mightily.

"Would I look this bent out of shape if I hadn't been in love with you that long? And by the way, it was falling for you that finally made me wise up about sex. So how come you didn't tell me?"

Eadie's brows went up. "When would have been a good time? Which reminds me, what about Celeste? You were upset about losing her.''

It wasn't because she didn't think he was being honest, but everything was falling too neatly into place for her not to have at least a tiny doubt. It was important to find out why, if he'd been in love with her as long as he'd said, he hadn't turned his masculine charm on her and simply asked her out years ago.

Now his cranky look returned. ''Is that a serious question, or are you going for one last torture? And when did I say I was upset about losing Celeste?''

''You were a bear for weeks after she broke off with you,'' Eadie challenged.

''I was a bear for weeks because I was tired of putting up with women I *didn't* want so I could prove something to the woman I *did* want. And I realized that all I'd managed to prove to you was that I was some kind of cowboy Casanova. Any man'd be testy over realizing he'd been that stupid for that long. Especially if he's doing without.''

Eadie giggled at the way he put it, and one corner of his mouth quirked sheepishly.

"And not too long ago, I was giving marriage advice to my best friend. How stupid does a man have to be to give advice about winning a woman when he doesn't have a clue about how to get the woman *he* wants?"

His half smile eased away and he went somber again. "I'm in love with you, Eadie. Crazy out of my mind with love for you." She lifted her palm to his lean cheek.

"I'm crazy in love with you, too, Hoyt. So much, I wasn't sure how long I could go without telling you. I didn't want to scare you away or make you feel obligated to say it to me if you didn't really feel it."

Hoyt's expression darkened. "Well, hell. Five years of two people dancin' around each other, eating their hearts out, isn't my idea of the way I want this marriage to go," he grumbled. Eadie smiled.

"It won't be that way now."

"At least I did one smart thing in all that time. The day I got hurt, I realized I'd had enough torture, that I was gonna figure out a way to get your attention. That's when I decided I had the perfect excuse to ask you to marry me. Whether you did or you didn't, at least I'd be put out of my misery.

I'd either get you to say yes, or I'd have to get past you.''

He gave her a swift, hard kiss and drew back. ''But marrying you wasn't enough. Then sex wasn't enough. I thought a woman like you might at least think you were in love if you had sex, or even that loving you senseless might make you say you loved me, if you did. Then tonight you were holding that baby and I wanted it all, everything a man and woman are supposed to have, but I realized we didn't have a right to make babies if both of us weren't in love.''

Eadie hugged him, so choked with emotion that it took her a moment to get at least some of it out before she could speak.

''Oh, Hoyt, I love you so much.'' She drew back to give him a teary glare. ''But I'm tired of talking.''

Hoyt tilted his head back to look down at her. ''So now I'm all talk and no action, huh? Well, lady, just remember when I'm lovin' the daylights outta you, that you're the one who tossed down the gauntlet.''

Eadie giggled as he closed in for a hot kiss that kindled a flash fire of sensuality that more than confirmed his macho boast about loving the ''daylights'' out of her. Tonight there were love words, feverishly given and received, then lavishly spoken in the age-old language of lovers.

Later, when they drifted in the gauzy clouds of contentment, they repeated those words in hushed whispers as they planned the years ahead and fell asleep dreaming of a future filled with loving each other...

In the next year, things at Webb Ranch slowly began to improve until the day it was suddenly put on the fast track to prosperity. The hasty compromise responsible for that fast track to prosperity was reached peacefully, considering the two headstrong personalities who negotiated it.

The trigger for that hasty negotiation and compromise was a positive reading on a home pregnancy test and a quick trip to the doctor to confirm it.

The first son in the next generation of Donovans arrived a few months later.